my year of
EPIC
ROCK

my year of
EPIC ROCK

ANDREA PYROS

sourcebooks
jabberwocky

Copyright © 2014 by Andrea Pyros
Cover and internal design © 2014 by Sourcebooks, Inc.
Cover design by Mike Heath
Cover photograph by Mike Heath

Sourcebooks and the colophon are registered trademarks of Sourcebooks, Inc.

Published by Sourcebooks Jabberwocky, an imprint of Sourcebooks, Inc.
P.O. Box 4410, Naperville, Illinois 60567-4410
(630) 961-3900
Fax: (630) 961-2168
www.jabberwockykids.com

Library of Congress Cataloging-in-Publication data is on file with the publisher.

Source of Production: Versa Press-USA, East Peoria, IL
Date of Production: July 2014
Run Number: 5001982

Printed and bound in the United States of America.

VP 10 9 8 7 6 5 4 3 2 1

For Leonard, Amelia, and John
I love you

Chapter

1

Nina, what are you doing?" Jackson said, his voice slightly muffled since it was coming from the tiny crack in the wood of my bedroom door. Startled, I jumped about five feet in the air.

"Stop spying on me!" I yelled back, flinging open the door, only to slam it again in my brother's giggling face.

"You are the weirdest human ever!" Jackson announced through the crack. "Mom says come down for breakfast," he added. Then I heard him walk off down the hallway.

I resumed my acrobatic twisting in front of my mirror— not because I'm some awesome gymnast, clearly, since I am *still* struggling on the cartwheel front, but because it was the only way to make sure my outfit looked good from all angles. I was confident the bright blue of my shirt— *cerulean*, my mom called it—looked pretty and matched the color of my eyes. And secretly, though I'd never say it to another living human being, I thought it fit well around the chest. Not too tight, but still, you could see that there was *something* underneath. Yeesh, finally!

But the jeans were tricky. Too skinny? Not skinny enough? I spun around one more time to try to see my butt. No luck. I could only catch a glimpse of me at a funny angle.

Normally Brianna would be my fashion expert, confirming that my first day of school outfit was suitably cute without giving off the dreaded "trying too hard" vibe. Usually she'd just come over, look through my closet, and pick out what I should wear, saving me the stress of doing it myself. "Besides, that way you can coordinate with what *I'm* wearing," she always said. I tried Brianna's cell one more time but it went right to voice mail.

"Ugh!" I groaned. I didn't bother leaving a message. Other than a few quick texts saying she was back, *finally*, from her family's monthlong trip to Italy, Brianna had been totally MIA since her return. I'd spent the summer doing a whole lot of nothing, punctuated by our annual not-at-all-exciting visit to my grandparents in Bethesda, so I'd been dying for her to get back starting about ten seconds after she'd left.

That weird ache in my stomach—the kind I get before my turn in kickball—returned. Something was definitely wrong. We talk, like, eighty-seven times in a twenty-four-hour period, even when it's not a super important day, like the start of seventh grade. For an occasion like today, we would probably just put each other on speakerphone for the whole morning.

I slid on my new red Chuck Taylor low-tops, pulled my brown hair up with a ponytail holder, and headed into the kitchen where Jackson was sitting and talking to Mom.

"Mom, what do you think?" I spun around slowly so she could see my outfit from all angles. It's not a good sign when the only people you can ask how you look are your mother and your dolt of a fourth-grader brother, but I wasn't in much of a position to be choosy.

Mom kissed me on the forehead. "Nina, you always look pretty," she said. The pencil she'd taken out of her mouth a moment before for kissing convenience went back in between her teeth. Which meant she was working on a new recipe for her latest cookbook and was busy taking notes.

"Mom, that does not help." I sat down at the counter and sighed.

The timer on our oven dinged, and Mom raced around our yellow kitchen, putting syrup and powdered sugar on the table, then sliding on her beloved candy cane–striped oven mitts, stained from years of spills and splatters. Mom had some flour in her short brown hair. How did that always happen?

"Ta-da!" Mom held up a platter of something and did a fancy-ish wave with her other hand. I rolled my eyes. I wasn't falling for that one. The last time she'd made a new dish and did the *ta-da!* move, the delicious-smelling cakey-looking thing turned out to be baked oatmeal. Want to guess who hates oatmeal? Me! Only my mother would make something that tastes like warm, soggy packing peanuts but smells as sweet as a cinnamon bun to fool her child into trying it.

"What is it?" Jackson asked her, looking interested.

"French toast. With no eggs, no dairy, and no wheat." She beamed.

I sighed. "Mom, isn't the whole point of French toast that it has eggs? What makes it French? Are you going to put a beret on top of it?"

Jackson laughed at my joke. Like, cracked up, holding his sides laughing. Though he laughs at *everything*, so I couldn't take it as a compliment on my comedy skills. If I'd somehow managed to rhyme *toast* with *fart* he'd fall off his chair.

"Try it before you make any comments," Mom said, ignoring me like always. Probably because I'm the choosiest member of our household, which I say means I'm the most sophisticated, so I'm usually skeptical. But since I'm also the only one with actual food allergies, Mom likes me to be her official tester for her cookbook series. If I hate it, it doesn't go in.

Oh, no, wait, I'm not the only one; Pepper, our basset hound, has food allergies too. She has to stay on a strict hypoallergenic diet or else she gets really gassy and her skin smells even worse than usual. Jackson thinks my special bond with Pepper is comedy gold, of course. He keeps saying maybe I was adopted from a pound. Ha ha ha. Jerk.

Mom served us each up a slice of the French toast, then sprinkled a bit of powdered sugar on top. She didn't even bother to offer me maple syrup, since I'd refuse to eat it today. Too messy!

Jackson, as usual, poured a giant glug out of it onto his plate and then dove into his breakfast. I took a tiny nibble. Actually, it wasn't bad, I had to admit. I ate another bite. Jackson was already halfway through his second piece. Then he paused and looked at his hand.

"Hmm," he said. Mom and I ignored him.

"Hmm," he said again, louder. Then he made a big show of flipping his hand over a few times, peering at it, and saying "hmmmm" a final time.

"Hmm, what, *Doctor*?" I shot him a look. Jackson thinks fart jokes are funny. He'll happily eat anything offered to him, even those gummy booger candies—flavored to taste like snot—our cousin Oliver made him eat once on a dare. But his number-one favorite pastime? Diagnosing himself with weird diseases. Mom and I like to pretend we don't notice, but this summer for his birthday, Dad picked up a bunch of used textbooks on anatomy, infectious diseases, and other medical stuff from the college campus where he works and wrapped them up for Jackson, who claimed it was "his best present ever." Mom was super mad about that. No muffins for Dad for a week.

"Does my skin look kind of weird here?" Jackson held his hand out for me to see and pointed at a spot that looked exactly like the rest of his skin.

"Everything about you looks weird," I replied. "I don't need to stare at your hand to know that."

Jackson grabbed his copy of *Current Diagnosis and Treatment in Infectious Diseases* and started flipping through it, nodding his head and rubbing his chin like Dad does when he's grading papers. Mom gave me a look and shook her head to remind me not to say anything else.

Please.

Like I was dying to discuss E. coli or hantavirus—a

disease Jackson has been obsessed with ever since we caught a mouse in our basement—or whatever else my brother had on his pea brain.

"So, when will Brianna be here?" Mom asked me. Every year, from third grade on, Brianna's parents dropped her off at our house so she and I could walk to school together, since we lived less than a half mile away. Totally walkable on nice days.

Suddenly my French toast was dry and rubbery in my mouth. I put down my fork.

"Oh, I think I'll just see her there," I replied, looking away. Mom didn't get the hint.

"But, aren't you going to—"

"I don't want to talk about it!" I jumped off the kitchen stool and went back to my room. I took my phone out of my pocket to make sure I hadn't missed any calls by accident. Nothing.

"Nina, are you ready?" Mom spoke quietly through my door. "Do you want to walk to school with Jackson?" I didn't, really, but I didn't have much of a choice. I put on my backpack, adjusting the puffy straps. My first day as a seventh grader and instead of arriving with my best friend, I was showing up with my little brother. How could this be anything but a very bad sign?

Chapter 2

The walk to school isn't very far, but it was long enough for me to realize I was totally worried about my first day. Mom says I have a nervous stomach and to ignore it, but this was more like how my stomach felt after I got off the Alien Abduction ride at the county fair. Jump. Thud. Lurch. I couldn't even get annoyed with Jackson for bumping into me—on purpose—every three feet because I was too busy chewing my fingernails and trying not to throw up.

Even though it was still warm outside, there were a few trees with leaves turning red and gold, and none of our neighbors were outside mowing their lawns the way they were, like, every morning during the summer. It was definitely fall and back-to-school season, normally my favorite time of year.

We reached the front of the elementary school just as the buses were opening their doors and all the kids rushed out. Jackson saw his friend Will and headed off in his direction while I veered left toward the entrance to our town's middle school right next door.

The people who built the Woodgrove Middle School designed big common areas in the lobby where students are allowed to hang out before the first bell. It's crazy loud sometimes—especially on the first day back or when everyone is about to leave for winter break or summer vacation.

When I got inside, I scanned the large room. The seventh graders tend to hang out up against the side wall where there are big looping, circular benches to sit on. It's a much better spot than the front of the room right by the doors where we were stuck last year as lowly sixth graders, but not as good real estate as the awesome area in the back behind a bunch of big plants that is exclusively for the lucky eighth graders.

Then I heard a totally recognizable laugh. *Brianna!*

I walked over to her, intent on finding out what was going on, but as I got closer, the neon green wrapper in her hand caught my eye.

It was a package of Nutty Buddies.

Wait, what? Nutty Buddies!?! Brianna shook a few of the candies into the palm of her hand, then passed the bag over to Shelley Abrams. Maybe Brianna heard my giant gulp or the sound of my stomach dropping to the floor, because she turned around and looked right at me.

"Oh, hi, Nina," Brianna said, in a super-casual, "We're kind of friends, right? I forget" tone, barely looking away from Shelley. There was an awkward pause before she jumped up to give me a quick hug with just the tips of her fingers. It felt more like she was trying to bump her shoulders to mine and avoid touching any other part of me.

She sat down again just as fast. Brianna was wearing jean shorts and a white tank top with a lace decoration on front, and arm warmers—one was striped, the other a sweatshirt-y gray. Everything about the outfit was new. Or at least I'd never seen any of it before.

I stood very still, a smile pasted to my face. "Um, when did you get back? How was Europe?" I asked, as casually as I could, even though I could feel my cheeks get all warm. That was my best friend, the one who'd sworn she'd rather die than eat a peanut if I couldn't, sitting and munching on Nutty Buddies.

"Oh, a few days ago!" Brianna answered and flipped her dark red hair which had gotten noticeably longer since I'd seen her last, or maybe it was just long because she'd straightened it so it lay totally flat, instead of styling it the way she usually did, which was to let it dry naturally, leaving it wavy and normal-looking. Not shampoo-commercial-straight at 8:00 a.m.

"It's been so busy, I'm sorry I didn't call you. Did you get my postcard? It was great! It was so crazy because in Venice we were having dinner and Shelley was sitting there at the next table over with her mom. Insane, right?" Brianna was giggling, and she and Shelley were passing the candy bag back and forth. Then Shelley put it on the seat between them.

The seat I could see was not being saved for me.

"Yeah, insane," I replied quietly. I reminded myself to swallow and tried to keep my smile up. I could barely manage it.

Brianna noticed me eyeing the Nutty Buddies. "Do you mind, Nina?" she waved her hand at the bag like she was shooing it away. "They're soooo yummy, but if you mind, I can put it away."

She turned to Shelley. "Nina's got a *massive* peanut allergy and kind of freaks out when they're around."

"I do not," I said. Had she *really* just said that? "Anyway, it's fine. Whatever. Glad Italy was fun…that sounds so cool…I can't believe you guys saw each other there…at the next table…wow."

But of course I minded. It's not like Brianna could

possibly have forgotten all the times she was there when my mom lectured me about being safe around food and how I had to always read ingredient labels to make sure there were no eggs or peanuts in anything. And how I have to pack my own boring cupcakes when I go people's birthday parties, instead of being able to have dessert with everyone, because just about everything delicious seems to be made with eggs or nuts or both. How I'm always kind of wondering if I'm taking my life in my fork if I eat anywhere but home.

Yes, I did mind.

A lot.

How could Brianna not know that?

"What happens if you eat a peanut anyway?" Shelley asked.

I turned to her—I'd been so transfixed by Bri I hadn't really focused on her before. Same Shelley as ever—hair totally shiny and halfway down her back without any of the annoying frizzies I seem to get from the warm, late summer air. Stylish clothing too. She was wearing short brown boots with a heel and what looked like a new pair of jeans. Shelley is the only seventh grader I know who actually looks like the girls do in shows about adorable boys who turn into werewolves or vampires and the girls who love them.

Brianna and I had spent so much time last year wondering about Shelley, who was a transfer student. Because she was new, and we live in a dinky small town in upstate New York, Shelley's freshness made her someone everyone wanted to be seen with.

Shelley spent most of her sixth grade hanging out with all the kids a grade older. She even supposedly *dated* one of them, a totally cute boy named Sebastian, who we speculated about endlessly. Neither Bri nor I had ever been on an actual date, let alone multiple dates, or even kissed anyone. Sebastian gave Shelley a gold bracelet—a real one—for her birthday, or at least that was what we'd heard.

We'd also heard Shelley dumped him at the end of the school year and stopped hanging out with Sebastian's twin sister, Maxie, her former best friend, at the same time, like she was over both of them. And that Sebastian was so upset he cried for, like, a week and refused to go to tennis camp.

I have no clue what was really true, but it all sounded exciting, and not like my life at all.

Shelley and Brianna were both looking at me, waiting for me to answer about what would happen if I ate peanuts. I looked down at the floor, uncomfortable with their stares.

"I'm not sure. I could get sick, I guess," I said, after a long pause. I didn't really want to talk about it.

"Oh, that must be such a hassle!" Shelley said. "I would *die* if I couldn't eat what I want, when I want it."

Cringe. Pity is the worst.

"Yeah, well, it's not a huge deal," I replied. Actually, it was, because I was the one who could actually die from anaphylactic shock, not die by exaggeration.

"Yeah," Brianna said, getting back to her original story. "We saw Shelley and her mom right next to us; it was so crazy!"

Again with the crazy. I got it.

She looked at Shelley, not at me, when she was talking—like she was waiting for Shelley's approval.

Shelley giggled and jumped in, "So we hung out the next few days. Our parents even let us go off alone one afternoon for lunch. You wouldn't believe how cute Italian guys are. They are *such* flirts."

"We were, like, followed, by this one gorgeous guy over a canal bridge." Brianna added, almost shrieking with laughter.

I wasn't sure why being followed was so wonderful. After all the years of lectures about safety and stranger danger, I thought anytime someone was following me it was time to head into a store or find a police officer. But I guess in Venice the rules were different and being chased around by a person you don't know is a good thing.

I was surprised that I was being so calm, standing there listening to Brianna talk. Brianna, the one I spent every weekend with, talked on the phone with every night, the one who'd spent nights at my house, and vice versa for the past four years, was acting like I was some random person who just came up to talk to her, instead of her closest friend in the world.

I looked down again at the telltale bright boogery green candy wrapper she was still holding, wondering whether the toxic peanut dust was heading toward me. I know my mom exaggerates the dangers of all things nuts, since I'm walking around on the planet every day surrounded by nut-eating citizens and I am fine, but on the other hand, it's not like I want to roll around in crumbs of the stuff, either.

I looked up at the big clock on the wall to check the time. There were only a few minutes until class started, but I couldn't stand there faking that everything was okay for even ten more seconds without bursting into tears.

"I'm going to run to the bathroom. I'll see you upstairs," I said, turning and racing off, not even waiting for them to reply. I heard Shelley call "*Ciao!*" after me, and then Shelley and Brianna resumed talking and giggling about something. I couldn't hear well enough to know what. I'd bet it was about Italy, where I've never been and will probably never get to go, or something else I wasn't a part of.

I just hoped I'd make it to the stalls before anyone saw that I'd started crying.

Chapter

3

The bathroom was cold, like it is whether it's June or January, and the doors to the stalls were freshly painted with a bright new coat of red paint the exact shade of a fire engine. When I locked the door behind me, I noticed the paint still felt a little tacky, like it hadn't totally dried. I'd probably get it all over my clothing, because my day wasn't already the worst ever. No one else was in the bathroom—a minor miracle, since it was usually super crowded with lip gloss–toting eighth graders, but everyone must have been too busy hugging friends and catching up.

Everyone but me.

Class would be starting soon. Time to pull it together. I sniffled and blew my nose on a big wad of toilet paper, and then washed my hands and used a wet paper towel to dab my eyes. I've never been able to hide it when I get upset—my eyes seem to stay red for the rest of the day—but I hoped everyone would be too preoccupied to really stare at me. It's not like Brianna would notice. She barely turned her head in my direction before.

I opened the restroom door and peeked my head out. There wasn't anyone standing outside by the water fountain right between the boys' and girls' bathrooms, so that meant no one could have overheard my snuffling and nose-blowing.

Whew!

Except I forgot to check the other direction, and as I snuck out of the bathroom, I walked right into someone's shoulder.

"Whoa!" the someone said, taking a big step backward.

I looked up and saw shoulder. Then I looked up some more. The someone was Ethan Chan, at least six inches taller than he was in June, the last time I'd seen him.

"Ethan, I'm sorry." I blushed. Red cheeks. Red eyes. Possibly red somewhere on my shirt—or worse, my butt—from the paint in the bathroom. I was sure I looked like a disaster.

"No problem," Ethan said.

We stood there awkwardly for a minute, then he asked, "Uh, so, who did you get for homeroom?"

"Mrs. Cook. You?"

"Me too. Cool. Um." He kind of shrugged. Then he

lifted his chin in the general direction of the stairs. Then he looked at me. I figured he wanted to get going.

"I'll see you up there," I said to him and then started walking. He did too. Right next to me.

I took a quick peek at Ethan out of the corner of my eye. Cargo shorts. Striped black and white polo shirt with a surfer guy on the front. Black flip-flops. Mostly I noticed that not only did Ethan seem taller, but he seemed muscley-er too. His dark hair was longer than last year— you could see how wavy it was now that it hit an inch or so below his ears. It looked messy in a good way.

I felt warm and kind of weird. Maybe I was getting sick? Where was Jackson and his medical textbook when I actually needed him?

When I was in kindergarten, Ethan Chan was my best friend. He would come over to my house at least once a month for a sleepover and my mom would make special magic noodles for us. Actually they were just plain old nothing magical about them beef and macaroni and tomato sauce, but Mom said they were magic and that you couldn't eat them without giggling. She was right about that part. Ethan and I wouldn't be able to finish our meal without laughing ourselves silly. Then Ethan would put on his Thomas the Tank Engine pajamas and I'd put on my puppy dog–themed nightgown and we'd go to bed. By first grade though, the boys and girls didn't hang out so much and that was it for Ethan and the Thomas pj's. I don't think he'd want anyone to know he used to wear those. They even had feet.

Ethan was quiet all through the lobby and up the two flights of stairs to Mrs. Cook's classroom. I kept trying to figure out something to say, but I was silent too. As soon as we got to the door to our classroom, he darted in with a quick "see ya" and a lift of the chin in my direction. I smiled goofily back at him.

Then I caught sight of Brianna sitting next to Shelley, and my smile was gone. I had conveniently forgotten until just then that Shelley was going to be in our homeroom this year. At our school, your homeroom teacher is also your first period teacher, so you wind up taking social studies with them or English, or whatever. Our school isn't very big. It's not *tiny* tiny, but it's not like we have thousands and thousands of students. Everyone knows everyone, pretty much.

After Brianna learned Shelley had supposedly broken Sebastian's heart and that she'd be in Mrs. Cook's class with us, Bri talked about her endlessly, even more than she had before. Like, to the point it was kind of boring.

Brianna was totally hoping Shelley would want to hang out with us this year. I said that maybe she might be too stuck-up or too shy or just too busy with all the other people who wanted to be with her, but that made Brianna mad and she told me not to jinx it.

I went and sat down in a chair next to Brianna. I couldn't really think of where else to go—it was so a part of our routine to be glued together that on the fly I couldn't begin to fathom another option. Brianna and Shelley kept up their conversation, and then Mrs. Cook walked briskly into the room. She looked around and everyone stopped talking immediately. We weren't idiots; she was famously strict, the strictest seventh grade teacher—maybe the strictest teacher in the whole entire school.

No one wanted to be the first to get Mrs. Cook's dreaded laser beam look of death students imitated when she wasn't around. Kids said she could hold the stare for a full minute without blinking even once.

Mrs. Cook wrote her name on her projector and it appeared up on the white board, and then she started talking about our year ahead. I tried to listen—I even got out my new notebook and fancy roll-y pen that I "borrowed" from my dad's desk, but I couldn't help but be distracted by Brianna and Shelley. They weren't doing anything—they were sitting quietly like the rest of us, but I was so focused on them it was like a noisy car alarm was going off next to me.

I slunk lower into my seat. Was anyone staring at me? Did anyone notice that everything about me was completely, totally, awfully different?

Chapter

4

I sat there and wondered how I was going to make it through the next seven hours. Then I remembered that, thankfully, I didn't have to. School always dismisses early on the first day of classes, right at 10:30. It's kind of a joke of a day, but at least I didn't have to deal with lunch.

Ugh, lunch!

I'd eaten lunch with the same person every single day for years: Brianna. Except if one of us was sick or the time in fifth grade that Brianna got to take an entire week off school to go with her grandparents to their timeshare in Hawaii.

At our school, we have a special table in the cafeteria set aside for kids with food allergies that everyone calls the peanut-free table even though it's for all allergies, not just nuts. It's cleaned off carefully between every lunch period, and the lunch aides stroll around and check on the people sitting there, although I'm not sure they would even know what to do if one of the kids got sick, except run and get the nurse or stand there and panic.

I used to sit at the allergy table when I was younger, but when I got to fourth grade, Brianna convinced me to convince my parents that if I didn't get to eat with her wherever we wanted, I wouldn't eat at all. At first Mom was completely against it, but I heard Dad trying to persuade her when they thought I wasn't listening. He almost never pushes Mom when it comes to anything that has to do with my allergies, but I guess that's because he saves all his fight for when he really disagrees with her. Finally, Mom gave in. As long as I always only ate food from home. As long as I promised—swore up and down—never to trade anything in my lunchbox for someone else's food. "Not even a banana!" Mom said, about a thousand times.

I don't even really like bananas.

But it was fine. Nothing bad ever happened. I always sat with Brianna, and she terrorized anyone who wanted to sit near us into leaving their peanut butter and jelly or egg salad sandwiches in their bags, or at least shamed them into eating at the other end of the table. I just sat there, doing nothing, and watched as she bossed everyone around. Talk about easy!

Also, you know what looks really gross? Egg salad.

Those few hours in Mrs. Cook's class felt endless, but finally the bell rang for dismissal. I made a big show of very slowly putting things away in my bag and ducking my head, even pretending to sharpen an already sharp, brand-new pencil so I'd seem busy and wouldn't have to catch anyone's eye. I didn't want people to notice my friendless state.

When I finally looked up, Brianna was gone. Shelley too. I was one of the last people in the room. I waited another minute and then walked out of class and out of the building as quickly as I could without breaking into a run. I didn't stop until I hit my house.

It was quiet inside when I let myself in, dropping my bag, shoes, and keys all in a pile on the floor by the front door. Sometimes on our first day of school, my mom is home and so is my dad if his teaching schedule allows it, so there're a lot of questions about how it went and what happened and all that. But Mom had reminded me earlier that she had to take Jackson to a dentist appointment and Dad was on campus, so it was just me and Pepper.

I turned on the computer we have in the corner of our kitchen and thought about trying to chat with someone, but I was the first one home, so there wasn't anyone around. And who would I even try to contact? I wasn't all that close with anyone else anymore, because I'd seriously spent so much time with Brianna. She and I used to hang out sometimes with Jody Fernandez and Chrissy Russo, and I had actually been tighter with Jody before Brianna came along, but then somehow it just got easier for Bri and me to pair up, and I spent less and less time with Jody and Chrissy. Not to be mean, exactly. It just somehow happened.

I moped my way up to my room, aimlessly, stopping to look at my leopard print–trim bulletin board. It was filled with all sorts of stuff—funny cartoons, a "Well-behaved Women Seldom Make History" bumper sticker that Grandma gave me, Dad's ticket to a Nirvana show back in 1993, a photo of me drumming from the summer I went to *Girls! Rock! Camp!*

But most of all it was filled with pictures of me and Brianna being silly together. I felt like the way girls feel in songs when they sing about a boy leaving them. How come no one ever sings a song about a friend leaving you for a newer friend? This had to hurt as much as a romance ending, right? Or maybe a guy breaking your heart *was* worse. In which case, remind me never, *ever* to fall in love.

I had the impulse to pull every photo of Brianna down and rip them all to shreds, but I couldn't bear to do something so…final. And then I had a brilliant idea: I should try to *talk* to her instead of acting like it was the end of the world.

It was understandable that she was excited about her big trip to Italy and getting to know Shelley, especially since Brianna had been so obsessed with her the whole previous year. That didn't mean she thought I was suddenly a worthless speck of dirt.

The achy feeling I'd had since this morning eased up a bit. I didn't want to text her. Private was the way to go. I checked the time. Brianna's bus would have dropped her off at home by now. I almost ran back to the computer. There was a green circle next to her name. She was home!

"Are you there?" I typed. My words stayed in the window for a second…then two. Still nothing. Three…silence.

Then she wrote back, "Here but on the run TTYL." The green circle next to her name turned gray, and the screen read, *Brianna is offline. Messages you send will be delivered when Brianna comes online.*

Ugh.

I put my chin in my hands, covered my eyes, and started to cry. Again.

I don't even know how long I stayed like that, but I didn't look up until there was a jangle of keys in the front door and I heard Jackson asking Mom how the dentist was so positive that Jackson didn't have a tooth abscess, since he definitely had a bitter taste in his mouth.

"Like a salty lemon," he explained, his words sounding garbled because he probably had his mouth wide open to show her. Typical Jackson.

Mom sighed deeply and ignored him. They came into the kitchen and she noticed me sitting in front of the computer.

"Oh, good, Nina, there you are," Mom said, walking toward me. "Since you're both home, I wanted to go through your piles of clothing from the summer and see what you've outgrown so we can give it away."

Then she noticed my teary face. "What…?" she said.

I turned my head away from her.

"I'm fine," I said, wiping my eyes on my sleeve.

"What's wrong, honey? Did something happen at school?"

Jackson raced over to stare at me. "Your eyes are all red."

"Yeah, thanks. I know. I look like a big, stupid, ugly loser!" I yelled and stood up. The chair rolled back onto Jackson's foot.

"Ow!" he yelled.

I didn't even say sorry as I raced up to my room. I heard Mom calling my name, but I ignored her and slammed the door behind me as hard as I could. Of course it's about as thin as a piece of cardboard so the slam sound isn't very dramatic. I wished it had made the loudest, most awful sound in the world.

Amazingly, considering my mother's personality—laid-back and hands-off is so not her style—she didn't follow me and insist I talk to her, so I spent the next hour lying on my bed with the pillow over my face. It was past noon when she knocked on my door to see if I wanted lunch.

"No, thanks," I yelled through the pillow.

"Nina, come on, have something. I made lasagna." Mom was trying to sound pleasant and calm, even though I'd bet she was frustrated that I wasn't telling her what was going on.

"I'm not hungry," I yelled back, even though my stomach was telling me otherwise. The last thing I'd eaten was a sliver of French toast at breakfast.

"You have to eat," Mom said, more firmly this time.

"I will. Later."

She didn't say anything else and walked away. I waited until I was sure that Mom and Jackson were done with lunch before going into the kitchen and making myself a plate of leftover lasagna.

"Warm it up first!" Mom called out from some other part of the house. How did she know what I was doing anyway? I gritted my teeth and took the plate back to my room—something that totally bugs Mom—without heating it up. It didn't taste all that great cold, and I was half nauseated, but I took a few forkfuls anyway.

I spent the day doing nothing except walking past the computer every few minutes, hoping Brianna's green dot would reappear. I tried to chat with a few other girls, like Alexis McCann and Jody, both of whom only asked where Brianna was once, but the whole time I just felt awkward and weird. A huge *thing* was missing.

I used to think it was so funny that everyone was always saying how Brianna and I were inseparable. Her mom called us "two peas" when we hung out at her house. Brianna was "pea one" and I was "pea two" and everyone at school—even adults—always asked me, "Where's Brianna?" if I went anywhere without her. But it was still a shock to realize how little time I'd spent with other people. If I had known that "Best Friends Forever" meant "Forever, or Just Until a Cooler Best Friend Shows Up," I would have made more of an effort to branch out.

I sat down with Mom, Dad, and Jackson for dinner that night, even though I didn't really want to. But refusing to come to dinner is not really an option in our house, unless you're sick, like sick with strep throat and a fever and a weird rash in the shape of Canada, not just sick with a cold.

I saw Mom giving Dad a *look*. Yep, they'd been talking about me.

Dad said, "How was your day, honey?" in a fake, overly enthusiastic way. He was, like, the worst actor ever.

My mom's eyebrows were going up and down like she was sending him a secret code. The two of them were ridiculous.

I made a big show of pointing to my mouth and how I was still chewing my chicken, and then I took a giant sip of water and wiped my mouth on a napkin before finally answering, "Fine."

"Were your teachers nice?" Mom asked me.

I shrugged, "No clue. We were only there for a few minutes."

There were a few more totally boring questions: "Do you think that Mr. Dwyer will start with kickball in gym?" "Were your new sneakers comfortable?" "Did Mrs. Cook mention how much homework you'll be getting?" "What day do you have art class?" But I sat and ate and didn't talk so much as grunt and mumble, and after a while everyone stopped trying to get me to chat it up with them.

Jackson was happy enough to tell our parents about his day and the cool gadget that Will had with him that the teacher took away because it was too loud. For my brother, that's really big news. Admittedly, his day sounded a hundred times better than mine. At least it didn't end in tears or a state of friendlessness.

After dinner, I went back to my room and, standing on tiptoes on my desk chair, dug out Gingey, my old stuffed gingerbread man that I keep hidden in a box up high in my closet. He was missing his eyes and nose and was so matted he wasn't even soft anymore, and his fur was more of a dirty brown than chocolate brown.

I lay in bed holding him as tight as I could and cried until I finally fell asleep.

Chapter

5

The next morning when I woke up, I felt happy for about fifteen seconds, until *bam*, I remembered the day before—Brianna and her arm warmers, Shelley and the Nutty Buddies, the gray circle next to Brianna's name when she logged off. Worst day ever. I'd hit bottom. My only hope was that there was no other way to go but up.

But when I got to Mrs. Cook's room, I realized that it was possible I'd be stuck flailing around at the bottom for a while. It wasn't like anything had changed. Brianna wasn't waiting outside the classroom door for me the way she always used to. Instead, she was already inside, actually kneeling on the floor next to Shelley's chair so as to better look up to her, laughing and waving her hands around like she was telling an exciting story. I caught a few words like "cross-eyed," "loser," and "worst outfit ever!"

But I sat down next to them again and tried for a big smile. "Hi!" I said. I waved a giant, "I'm on a Thanksgiving Day Parade Float" kind of wave.

"Hi, Nina," Shelley said to me, flashing a huge, hard-to-believe-it-was-real grin. Maybe she was part robot.

"Yeah, hi, Nina," repeated Brianna. No smile there, not even a fake one. Or much in the way of eye contact.

Then Brianna resumed her conversation, quieter this time. She was either deliberately trying to keep me from hearing or just didn't realize I was shut out. I unzipped my backpack and peered in as if there were a very important item at the bottom. If I'd been able to dive in headfirst and zip it back up around me to avoid having to witness Brianna suck up to Shelley, I would have.

The whole spectacle was the grossest.

Mrs. Cook came in and took attendance, then started in on her lecture about the three branches of government. When the bell rang, she sent us on our way to second period.

"Bye," I called to Shelley and Brianna, hoping my tone was just casual enough.

They looked at me blankly.

"See you at lunch," Brianna said back absentmindedly over her shoulder.

Wait! Did she want me to sit with them?

"Totally!" I said way too happily, like I'd won a million dollars. I almost skipped to math class. I replayed the moment in my mind all the way down the hall.

Maybe I had done something to make Brianna mad and now she wasn't upset anymore. I bet she'd say something to me—it's not like Brianna ever kept her opinions to herself. Once in fifth grade I told Alexis that Brianna thought Thomas Aronstein was a good athlete—which he is, everyone knows that!—and Brianna was so mad she screamed at me and then didn't talk to me for, like, almost a week, because she said it made it seem like she had a crush on Thomas. Which she did. In order to get her to talk to me again, I had to apologize about twenty times and buy her a "Forgive Me" card from the drugstore.

I still don't think I did anything wrong.

Would Brianna, Shelley, and I have sleepovers now, all three of us? Maybe Shelley was a lot nicer than I thought. Shelley was probably just cautious with new people because everyone judged her for being so pretty and because everyone made such a big deal out of her when she moved here.

I wondered what her house was like. Would she want to come over after school with Brianna some time? Would it be weird to have snacks after school? What if snacks were so not seventh grade? All that thinking about food made me wish I had a slice of blueberry buckle cake.

After math was over, it was time for language arts with the ancient Miss Teitlebaum. She was so old that I know *parents* of kids in my grade who had her as a teacher. Miss Teitlebaum had what looked like one long strand of hair wrapped around her head in a big circle. Also she smelled like corn on the cob. One time I heard she fell asleep during class and no one woke her so she was still snoring when the bell rang.

After my morning classes finally wrapped up, I went to my locker to get my lunch bag and headed into the cafeteria as quickly as I could. The sixth graders were only halfway through their allotted eating time, and they were yelling and acting totally immature. I saw one boy sneak up and wipe his hand on the back of a girl's shirt and then race back to a group of other boys, laughing and pointing.

The seventh graders were just filing in. I looked around and caught sight of Brianna, who was searching the room for someone. Was it me? We hadn't staked a claim to our table yet.

I walked over to her, smiling.

"Oh, hi, Nina," Brianna said, but she didn't really even look at me.

No. It wasn't me she'd been looking for.

"Hey, Brianna," I said hesitantly. "Is everything okay? You know? Like, in general? Are you mad at me?"

She looked uncomfortable and almost annoyed.

"Of course everything is totally fine. It's all good. Have you seen Shelley? Oh, wait! There she is! Shelley!" Brianna raced over to Shelley and gave her a huge hug and pointed to the table near where she'd been standing. She pulled Shelley over by the hand.

"I saved us seats," Brianna said to her. I sat down at the table and put my brown paper bag in front of me too.

"Oh, awesome," I said, even though she hadn't said a word about saving *me* a seat. I hoped it was because she just assumed I'd sit with them, but deep down, I realized I was being pathetic. Brianna was crystal clear about telling people what she wanted. It's not like she'd transformed into a new, less bossy or opinionated person after a month in Italy. If she'd wanted me to sit with her, she would have invited—no, insisted—that I join them. She wasn't insisting because she didn't care.

Great.

"Let's go buy lunch," Shelley said, dropping the striped hoodie she'd tied around her waist down on the bench. "Are you coming?" Shelley asked me.

I pointed to my lunch. "No, I'm all set."

The two of them walked off to wait in the cafeteria line together, not even looking back at me once.

"Yeah, see you guys," I mumbled, taking out my pretzels

and hummus and crumpling my stupid babyish paper bag into a ball. My lunch looked seriously unappetizing.

I watched all my classmates inching forward in line, waiting for their lunches. It seemed like forever before Brianna and Shelley finally came back with their trays, laughing and giggling as they sat down, Shelley next to me, Brianna directly across from her.

"It would be awesome, right?" Shelley said. "Right?" she turned to me.

"What would?" I looked back and forth at both of them, confused.

"Tell Brianna she has to help me throw a big party for Halloween. There's nothing else to do around here except for that joke of a talent show," Shelley said. "And hardly anyone goes to that."

Brianna didn't look at me—she was too busy staring at Shelley.

"Oh, yeah, a party sounds awesome," I mumbled, jamming a pretzel into my mouth.

"We could come up with a funny nickname for us. Sheliana's Massive Party? Brelley's Big Bash?" Shelley said. "You'd come, right, Nina?"

She turned back to Brianna, shrieking excitedly. "We have got to get that mint chip gelato like we had in Italy!

I'm so sure my mother can find it for us in the city." She put her hand under her long hair and flipped it back over her shoulder. A strand got stuck on my lower lip. Ick.

She turned to face me again, and I tried to lean away from her in a non-obvious way—I didn't want another mouthful of hair.

"Do you eat gelato, Nina?" She stared at me. "It's kind of like ice cream. Only way better."

"I'm not sure. I've never had it." I felt my face get hot and red. "It sounds great though."

"Oh my god, gelato is soooo good. But it probably has eggs, so *she* couldn't eat it," Brianna said, flicking her wrist in my direction.

I wanted to feel like I was part of the conversation, instead of sitting there dopily, so I said, "Actually, I love smoothies. Brianna and I both do, right?"

Shelley looked at me kind of confused—she lifted up both her brows super high, like maybe she didn't understand what I was saying and was waiting for me to clear things up. I felt like the biggest dolt.

Why had I just said that?

Yes, Bri and I sometimes get smoothies at Kickin' Koffee, but it wasn't, like, our official drink or anything.

Brianna seemed embarrassed. She made a frustrated

"gaaaa" sound with her breath, pushing the air out of her mouth.

"Yeah. I mean, they're fine," she rushed in, shrugging. "But I'm into macchiatos now. They're a million times better."

There was another awkward pause.

"Remember that hot guy working at the gelato place?" Shelley started laughing and Brianna did too. They tried to tell me their "hilarious" story about the gorgeous Italian guy who was so much older who flirted with them, but they were laughing so hard they could barely get the words out and wound up talking to each other instead of me.

I mean, I like hot guys too, but how was this so funny to them? They were acting the way Jackson does when he watches that commercial where a baby in diapers throws a baseball and hits his dad in the crotch. Cracks Jackson up every time.

"Sorry, you must think we're so crazy!" Shelley wiped her eyes because she'd cried from laughing so hard. Then she looked down at her tray, which she hadn't even touched.

"This food is gross. I have so lost my appetite," and she shoved the tray to the other side of the table.

"Me too!" Brianna pushed her tray away right in mid-chew. I rolled my eyes. Brianna never loses her appetite. Served her right if she were starving.

I looked at the wall clock. Maybe the gods of time would smile down on me and the minute hand would hurry up and move so I could be done with sitting there. But no, of course not. Finally I stopped listening to them. I imagined that my face was flushed and blotchy, so I pressed my water bottle against it to cool myself off. It felt nice. The bell rang, and Shelley stood up fast, with Brianna popping up right after her.

Ethan walked by with some kids from his soccer team. He was barely out of earshot when Shelley whispered to Brianna, "Ethan got totally cute, right?" in the loudest voice a whisper can make, like she didn't mind at all if someone heard her. They both giggled again and were already walking off before they heard me call out, "Good-bye."

Chapter 6

"Hold this, Orlando," Mrs. Cook strode into our classroom the following morning with two jumbo-sized white plastic jars labeled "1" and "2"—they looked like they used to hold about fifty gallons of mayonnaise—and handed them to Orlando Rodriguez, who got so startled his glasses slid off his nose.

"Pick one piece of paper from each," she instructed him. "Tell us what each ones says."

Orlando reached in to the "1" jar. "Shane McCormick." Orlando looked over to where the new kid in school was sitting. Shane lifted up his hand and gave the class a "Yo."

Then Orlando pulled a scrap from the second jar. "*Tinker v. Des Moines.*"

Mrs. Cook handed the buckets to Shelley, who was sitting next to Orlando. Shelley unfolded her paper. "Ethan Chan," she read out loud and smiled at Ethan—all her teeth showing.

"Present," said Ethan. Shelley giggled and actually

blinked her eyelashes a bunch of times. She read the second scrap: "*Gideon v. Wainwright.*"

Mrs. Cook went around the room, letting the first half of the class pick names. As I waited for the bucket to get to me, I crossed my fingers that I'd get Brianna, but when I unfolded the little piece of paper, I saw that I'd picked Tiernan Albert instead.

"Tiernan." My voice sounded squeaky when I said his name out loud. "*Marbury v. Madison.*" I slunk lower into my seat as Mrs. Cook finished going around the seats, pairing up the whole class.

I had no clue what our teacher was planning, but already I didn't like it. Chrissy picked Brianna. Shelley was clearly psyched when she said Ethan's name—I would have been too. But I was stuck with Tiernan Albert! I had to admit, Tiernan was perfectly…fine. *And* super smart. He was just a bit different. He wore crazy hats and carried a rolled up comic book in his back pocket every day, and he and his friends all hung out after school and played some insane game that took about six *years* to finish. Years. Not hours.

Tiernan's mom and my mom were friends. When we were babies, they met at the park while Tiernan and I were on the swings. His mom has white hair even though she's not that old, and she leaves it long and loose and curly. It's really pretty. Mrs. Albert cracks my mom up. I can always tell when they're on the phone together, since my mom is usually not cracking up otherwise.

Still, I'd been hoping to get paired up with Brianna. But at least she wasn't with Shelley, so I could take comfort in knowing they weren't going to be plotting their social takeover of the school in the immediate future.

"Okay, move your seats around. Sit with your partner," Mrs. Cook instructed us, pulling out the chair from underneath Orlando so he almost fell backward. She didn't seem to notice. "Up! Up!" The room was filled with laughing and noise for a few minutes as we all got up to find a spot next to the right person.

"Hi, Nina," Tiernan said cheerfully. His reddish-brown hair was curly and wild and bushy, and he had on a black T-shirt that read, *Enjoy yourself. It's later than you think*. I didn't even understand what that meant.

"Hey," I replied. I felt like being rude because that was the kind of mood I was in. I had to force myself to smile—even though I could only manage a grimace.

Mrs. Cook cleared her throat—actually, she pretty much just said "Ahem," but with some extra throaty noise for added emphasis. Everyone stopped talking right away.

"What are these names you read out?" she asked. She looked around.

"Famous court cases?" Jody said.

"Yes, good, Jody. I paired you up for today's assignment. You're going to go together to the library to research the Supreme Court case you've been given, working together for the half hour to find out what you can about the case: what happened, who was the petitioner and who was the respondent, how the court ruled. I'll also want you each to pick a side—toss a coin to decide if you need to—and argue it for the class based on the arguments the attorneys made originally. If you don't agree with your side, that's fine. I just want to hear the key points made to the court. Got it?" A few people raised their hands, but she ignored them and sent us off to the library, reminding us to return when it had been thirty minutes.

"Don't make me come find you," she added ominously.

"Cool project," Tiernan said as he was gathering up his backpack. Maybe for him. But the idea of making an oral presentation to the whole class hardly seemed appealing to me.

"Come on," he said, motioning for me to follow him. "Let's grab a computer before anyone else does." We race-walked together to our school library, Tiernan laughing a fake evil laugh when we heard "Wait!" and "Hey!" calls from behind us.

"Suckers!" he yelled back as he swung open the glass library door, not at all sheepish when Mrs. Delaney, the librarian, looked up at him from behind her tall wooden desk.

"Hello, Tiernan," she said.

"Hey, Mrs. Delaney," he waved. "Sorry for yelling. We're here for Supreme Court research."

"Go find two chairs. I'll bring over my best books." She pushed her rolling chair back and stood up.

I gave Tiernan a glance. Mrs. Delaney wasn't normally that helpful with the rest of us. She thought we'd mess up her pristine space by actually using it.

"I'm here a lot after school," he said, shrugging, as we found a computer and sat down. "When my parents divorced last year, I started coming here to do my home-work and wait for my mom to get me after work." Then he shrugged again, in a *whatever* kind of way.

"That's…that must have been…I didn't know…" I trailed off, unsure about what to say. I know a ton of people get divorced, but it's still a bummer when it happens. Plus it makes me all paranoid about my own parents.

"Yeah, it was lame at first. Now I'm used to it. It's not

so bad. Everyone told me about the double presents I'd score for my birthday, and they were right."

Tiernan started typing, but I nudged him aside. "Here, I've got it," I said.

I can't stand watching someone type. It's torture. I either have to turn my head away or do it myself because if they make a mistake or go too slow, I get all antsy and annoyed.

"How was your summer? Anything new?" he asked me.

"Eh, no, nothing new. Same old, same old," I said back, clicking on a link.

I was glad that Tiernan hadn't asked me anything about Brianna. It was possible he didn't notice that my best friend wasn't hanging out with me anymore, or he did notice and didn't care. Whatever the reason, I appreciated it.

He sneezed loudly. "Stupid tree pollen." Tiernan took a tissue out of his pocket and blew his nose. "Sorry."

"No problem. Gesundheit," I added. At least he was trying. When Jackson sneezes, he refuses to cover his mouth, and the only way he'll use a tissue is if we get one for him. He totally gets us to do it every time too—I'm not going to sit there and watch him drip snot around the house.

"Here," I said, pointing at the screen. "This site looks like it has a ton of stuff."

We sat there silently for a while, looking at the screen and reading the textbooks Mrs. Delaney had dropped off. Tiernan was taking notes at warp speed.

"Which side do you want to be?" I asked him.

"The winning one, obviously," he said.

"Hey, me too!" I laughed. "Rock, paper, scissors. Best out of three."

I could hear snippets from the other teams working on their projects. I tried to secretly scan around to see where Shelley and Ethan were or Brianna and Chrissy—I hoped all four of them weren't sitting together, having the world's most amazing time, making plans to hang out after school—but I couldn't find them.

Tiernan, on the other hand, didn't care who was sitting where, or who was teamed up together. He seemed… relaxed. Or oblivious, but it was relaxing being around him. I suddenly felt bad about the "Ronald McDonald" nickname Brianna had given him because of his curly hair. I'd always laughed whenever she whispered it as he walked by.

I hoped he'd never overheard us.

When the period was over, Tiernan and I packed up our research and hustled back to Mrs. Cook's classroom to finalize our strategy. The other groups trickled back in behind us and started doing the same. I noticed that Shelley was doing the hair flip thing a lot but it wasn't smacking Ethan in the face like she had me. He did have the height advantage though. Ethan seemed focused on her, listening and nodding as she talked. I wondered if he thought she was pretty. It would be weird if he didn't. *Everyone* thought Shelley was pretty.

"Nina? Over here." I turned to see Tiernan making a goofy face to get my attention.

Just then Mrs. Cook came over to us. "Ready?" she asked. "You two were first back, so why don't you start us off?"

She clapped to get the class's attention. "We'll get to the first few teams today and finish the rest tomorrow. Now give your full attention to Nina and Tiernan, please."

Gulp.

"We're totally, one hundred percent ready," Tiernan said. He sounded confident. "Nina's up first." He pointed at me. "Take it away, lawyer."

I tried to say something but it came out like a whispery croak. I took a deep breath and started again. I had to stare down at my notes the entire time instead of looking up, and I'm not sure I even paused to take a breath, but at least I got through my entire argument. When it was done, my heart was racing and my face was hot, but I'd made all my points and didn't stumble more than once.

Okay, maybe twice.

Tiernan went right after me. No squeaking. He sounded great, other than a mid-argument sneeze/nose blow, which I noticed made Brianna smirk and look over to Shelley to try to catch her eye. It felt weird seeing the things Brianna had always done—we'd always done—but that suddenly felt so much harsher witnessing them from a distance.

When we were finished, Mrs. Cook wrote something down in her notebook then looked up and actually smiled! "Excellent, excellent. You two have set a very high bar for the rest of the class."

Tiernan poked me in the arm and whispered, "Yes!"

I sat there, beaming.

After that, class was a lot less stressful. Tiernan and I sat back and looked smug. I didn't even snicker when Shelley read "Mr. Gideon Clarence" instead of "Mr. Clarence Gideon" and had to be corrected by Mrs. Cook.

I was surprised when the ball rang. I'd actually been having fun instead of trying not to cry for a change. Thanks, Marbury and Madison!

Chapter

7

I waved good-bye to Tiernan and got up, walking out the door just at the same moment as Brianna and Shelley.

"Good job," Shelley said to me, like she meant it. I was glad I only took a tiny bit of pleasure in her earlier mistake.

"Thanks. You guys did well too," I said, then said to Brianna, "Um, see you at lunch?"

"Oh, sure," Brianna replied, and then turned around to give Shelley a huge hug good-bye. No hug for me. It kind of took the thrill out of my big Supreme Court win.

I took a deep breath and thought about my dad's favorite joke anytime Jackson or I act like sore losers when we play a game. Dad yells, "There's no crying in baseball!" It's from a movie. Sometimes it works and we stop our complaining. One time I threw a Monopoly board at Jackson's head. There was a lot of crying that night. Thinking about Dad making his dumb joke always stops me from getting more upset. At least I could proceed down the hallway without looking all blotchy and watery-eyed.

At lunchtime, I decided I'd wait a bit longer to enter the cafeteria so I could be sure Shelley and Brianna were sitting down and I wouldn't be stuck there all by myself. By the time I strolled in, all casual-like, they were at a table together, of course, and laughing like always.

"Hi, guys," I said, putting down my bag and trying my best to sound friendly, not sulky. I didn't entirely pull it off.

"Tiernan sure got into the assignment today, didn't he?" Brianna said, looking at me and then back to Shelley. I wasn't sure what she meant, but she wasn't trying to be nice, that was for sure.

"Yeah, he's really smart," I replied. "I *wish* I was that smart."

"It makes up for his fashion sense," Brianna said.

"That's harsh," said Shelley and giggled. Unbelievable. A joke about his wardrobe. How original.

"Whatever," Shelley said. "I'm focused on our party anyway."

"Oh, yeah, your party, right. You guys are on it," I said. *Our* party. Ouch.

Brianna looked happy—like she'd accomplished something major. Since when was hosting a party a reason to be that proud? Buy chips, soda, and play music. Big freakin' deal! Try winning a case in front of the Supreme Court and then talk to me.

"I think we should ask Josh to come over early, to help us set up," Brianna said. "And maybe Ethan too, right?"

Josh Ricci is this teeny tiny guy in our grade with almost-white blond hair, and he's always tagging along after whomever he thinks is popular while making mean comments about everyone else.

Last year he got into some argument with Destiny Torres, and he pulled on her puffy coat so hard the sleeve ripped. And when we learned about Lake Titicaca in fifth grade, he didn't stop laughing for, like, the rest of the year.

Josh has always left me alone, but only because he hasn't come up with a good way to rhyme my name with a gross body part. Total jerk. I didn't think Ethan was really tight friends with him—Ethan usually hung out with more normal kids, like the ones on his soccer team, but maybe I was wrong, like I seemed to be about everything else lately.

"Totally. Let's have them come over *extra* early," Shelley drew out the word "extra" so it sounded like she was saying something she wasn't supposed to, then laughed like she'd made a super clever joke.

Hilarious.

Shelley opened up a tiny little Velcro sandwich bag with red swirls on the front and took out a dainty, perfectly unsmushed sandwich. How was that even possible?

My sandwiches always looked like they'd taken a cross-country ride on the back of a donkey by the time lunch rolled around.

She gave her food a dirty look. "I hate bringing my lunch to school, but my mom only had big bills and didn't want me taking a hundred dollars out of her wallet," she said. Then Shelley noticed my brown bag and added, "Sorry, Nina, I didn't mean that there's anything wrong with bringing your own food, if you're into it."

"That's okay." I didn't want her to see that I felt bad, although I couldn't seem to stop frowning. I felt like my lips were tugging down my entire face, all droopy basset hound style. Maybe that theory about how humans start to resemble their pets was really true.

I forced myself to smile. A big, fake one.

"Besides, who cares about lunch? It's the stupidest meal of the day anyway," I added.

No one said anything back.

Shelley took a bite from her sandwich. I noticed that it was peanut butter and jelly right away just from the smell.

My stomach clenched a little.

I realize that sitting near peanut butter is not a big deal. My mom and dad have told me that a billion times, although they follow that up with "So long as you don't eat it. Or touch it. Or look it directly in its eye." Ha ha. But it's weird when the person next to you is eating your own personal poison.

My cool uncle Mike who's a yoga teacher insists that I'm lucky that I have food allergies, because "at least you know what your Kryptonite is." I didn't feel very lucky at that moment.

I looked around the lunchroom. There was plenty of yelling and laughing and chewing and talking. Everyone seemed to be sitting where they were meant to be. Except me. I felt out of place.

I was *out of place.*

Shelley took another nibble from her sandwich. A dot of peanut butter covered the navy polish on one of her fingertips.

Was I getting a hive? I felt itchy all of a sudden. *Was I having an allergic reaction?*

I took a breath. I tried to remind myself that there wasn't any possible way I could have eaten anything I was allergic to, since I hadn't even put a finger near my lips, let alone taken a bite of food, but my body didn't believe me.

"I forgot to get my pen back from Tiernan from earlier. I'll see you later," I said, standing up. Brianna turned back to Shelley without a word, but that was okay, because I was freaking out and hoping my face wasn't puffing up and if it was, that neither of them noticed.

Brianna and I used to play the "Which is worse?" game a lot, like, "Which is worse: peeing your pants at school or being bitten by a hundred fire ants?" I couldn't decide which was worse—having an allergic reaction, or having a total panic freak out and looking crazy in front of the two people you most wanted to look cool around.

I could see Tiernan sitting over at the peanut-free table with some other kids. I wasn't even sure why I'd come up with him as my excuse. It was just his name was the first one that popped in to my mind. Maybe because I'd been with him all morning. Or maybe because I'd never seen him be anything but nice—ever—and I desperately yearned to be near a friendly face.

I hustled over, sitting down quietly at the very end of the bench, right next to Tiernan, without saying anything. I heard insanely loud laughter from Brianna and Shelley.

"Uh, yeah, I can pretty much guarantee that whatever they're talking about is not that funny," Tiernan said, looking at me and shaking his head.

I was so grateful I had to stop myself from hugging him. My breathing felt fine again. Go figure.

Tiernan was sitting next to Madison Sullivan, who

honestly used to cry every time someone even ate a peanut within twenty feet of her until, like, last year. And Pouty Heidi was there with them too, even though I didn't think she had allergies—she's just friends with Madison. Pouty Heidi isn't her real name—it's Heidi Burnett—but she never seemed to smile, so Bri and I called her Pouty Heidi behind her back all the time. The crazy thing was she looked like a young, just as pretty version of some famous Hollywood actress like Zoe Saldana. Heidi has big eyes and delicate features and a so-cute pixie haircut that would make me look like a boy.

If I had been her, I seriously would never *stop* smiling.

Shane was there too, the new kid.

"Nina, this is Shane," Tiernan said.

"Yeah, I know," I said. "Hi, Shane."

"Yo," he said back. He was wearing a faded orange T-shirt with the name of a band my dad listens to. It made his orange hair look even brighter.

He didn't have any food in front of him, just a red drink box. It had plain letters and no pictures of happy fruit tumbling around, the way normal juice boxes do.

"What's that?" I asked him, pointing to it.

"Oh, this is Tropical Punch Disgustingness. The other

flavors I sometimes drink are Lemon-Lime Vomit, and Cherry Dog Turd."

I gave him a look.

"I'm allergic to, like, everything," he explained. "But luckily for my taste buds, I can still enjoy these wonderful allergy-free, completely man-made, not found in nature nutrition supplements!"

He held it up before taking a big gulp and then making a fake gagging noise.

Tiernan was cracking up. "I used to drink those stupid things before I outgrew my dairy allergy. They do, in fact, all taste exactly like a small, rabid animal died and they marinated it in a rancid Creamsicle for a year and then strained it and served it to you with a straw."

Tiernan grabbed Shane's drink and waved it in Madison's face. "Want some?"

"Gross!" she yelled, leaning so far backward she was almost horizontal. "No, thank you."

It was impressive how Shane was so laid-back. If I couldn't have anything at lunch but a weird drink, I'd be bummed. He seemed not to care at all. I could take a few stress-busting pointers from him.

The lunch aides were clapping their blue-gloved hands, signaling it was time to start packing up our stuff to make room for the next grade. I walked out with Tiernan, making the hugest effort not to turn my head around to look for Brianna. Not looking, though, never works out for me, so of course in my quest to stare straight ahead I didn't even notice Ethan was standing next to me until I heard him say something to Tiernan.

"Ack!" I shrieked.

Very smooth, Nina.

Shelley and Brianna were right. Ethan did get cute. He got adorable. I'd caught myself staring at him a few times during class when I was totally, one hundred percent sure he wasn't looking my way, in between bouts of moping about Brianna ignoring me. My entire range of emotions lately had been mope, sulk, stare, stare, mope, mope some more, and pity myself.

Even Ethan's gray T-shirt with the slightly ripped collar looked cute on him. He had a dark blue baseball cap stuck into the back pocket of his jeans. That was adorable too.

He and Tiernan started talking about hanging out after school, and their wizards and spellcasters and a bunch of other stuff that made no sense.

I knew that Ethan hung out with Tiernan because they were neighbors. I didn't realize Ethan was into Tiernan's fantasy game madness though.

"How's your wizard, Nina?" Ethan said, cracking up.

"Very funny. I don't know what you guys are talking about."

"You could come hang out sometime and find out," Ethan said. "We'll teach you. It's not that complicated, and I bet you'd pick it up fast." He looked right at me. And smiled, in his totally friendly, always nice to everyone, Ethan way.

How come I never noticed how Ethan's dark hair curled behind his ears so it was the perfect kind of messy, or how gorgeous his skin looked? Not a bump or anything.

I was smitten.

Or was it smitted? Smited? Or was that when you get burned in a fire?

I couldn't believe we used to have sleepovers! I blushed and then got so flustered I didn't even know what to say about hanging out or anything. So I said nothing, of course. That seemed to be my theme of the week: Nina, the great wit.

But Tiernan dug into his bag and pulled out a video game, changing the subject and therefore saving me without even realizing it.

"Check this out," he said, handing it to Ethan.

"Oh, yeah, we're on," Ethan said back, giving Tiernan a very gentle punch on the shoulder.

Tiernan sneezed in response.

Tiernan had saved me from death by shame twice in the last thirty minutes. I owed him, big time.

"Seriously, you should hang out with us later," Ethan said.

Did he mean later as in *Come hang out with us later today?* Or like, *Let's hang in the very distant future when you stop acting so weird?* Before I could figure it out, Ethan slung his backpack over one shoulder and bounced off down the halls, leaving me feeling silly and tongue-tied and happier than I'd been in days.

Chapter 8

I thought about asking Tiernan what the deal was with his plans with Ethan but decided against it.

Too scary.

Scary if Ethan didn't want me to hang out, and doubly terrifying if he did. What would we talk about? Would I blow it?

Instead, I did what any mature young woman would do in my shoes: I avoided the entire issue and went straight home instead as soon as school let out.

It was a huge relief to walk inside. I was so exhausted from all the highs and lows of the day. I felt like I'd just been a contestant on a crazy reality show—like where you're given a ball of string and three sticks of gum and have to make it out of the jungle alive. Except my jungle was Woodgrove Middle School.

I couldn't wait to finally crash on my bed and listen to music for the rest of the afternoon and be by myself.

But when Jackson and I walked through our front

hallway, I noticed that the dining room table was set with the pretty bamboo place mats that we never use unless we have company—adult company, not, like, a friend of mine or Jackson's—and that the house smelled nice. Dinner party nice. There was plenty of noise coming from the kitchen too—banging and whisking and whirring.

"Hi, guys!" Mom said, coming out to the hall to greet us wearing her "All Hail the Chef" apron Dad gave her last year for Mother's Day.

"Do you want something to eat?" she asked us, adding, like always, "Wash your hands."

I rolled my eyes but walked over to the kitchen sink anyway. The school bus is epically gross, I admit. While the bus is waiting to pull out, the fifth grade boys like to play "Pull My Finger" and compete for the loudest, foulest fart bragging rights, and on Fridays they have a contest they call the "Hock-a-Loogie Olympics." Plus little Joe Frieburn throws up on the ride home every time the cafeteria serves chili. It is the worst.

I was halfway up the stairs to my room when Mom called out of the kitchen, "Nina? Nina? Come back."

I sighed and went back downstairs.

"What, Mom?" I said, eyeing the plate of chocolaty cookie bars on the counter. "What are those?"

"No-Bake 'Mocklate' Chocolate Energy Bars." She passed the plate toward me. "Try one."

I took a tentative bite. Tasty!

"It's for the book. I'm making a few new things to try out tonight. Shreya is coming over."

"Who?" I said, a crumb falling out of my mouth where Pepper was waiting, tail wagging, to snarf it up.

"Shreya. Dr. Mehta." Mom stirred something on the stove with a wooden spoon and put the lid back on. "Remember, I told you a few weeks ago that she was going to come over for dinner some night to talk about the cookbook?"

Dr. Mehta is my allergist. I go to her once a year for blood tests and to find out that, yes, big shock, I still can't eat peanuts or eggs.

"She's going to write the introduction." Mom was clearly excited—she was talking with her hands as much as her mouth. "This is a big deal. She's quite a well-known name in the allergy community, and—"

"Mom, really, she has to come over for dinner? Tonight? Is she going to want to give me a check-up or something while she's here?"

"Don't be silly. She's coming to eat. So she can try some of my food and we can talk about what she'll be writing."

"That's weird. No one else's doctor comes over to hang out. Doesn't she have better things to do?"

"Nina, I explained this. And I thought you liked Dr. Mehta." Mom sounded like she was only half listening to me.

"She's fine, Mom. But that doesn't mean I want to spend my free time with her. Sheesh!"

Dr. Mehta is nice and all, even though she used to be obsessed with whether I was eating enough and gaining enough weight and upping my protein intake and blah blah blah. Her office would make my parents bring me in twice a year to step on the scale. She may be a genius when it comes to allergies, but that was completely annoying. I'm scrawny. And short. So sue me!

Also she once suggested to my parents that they serve me mini meatballs on toothpicks to fatten me up, so I swear we used to have that for dinner five nights a week. If I never see a meatball again, it will be too soon. Memo to parents everywhere: Just because you cook something teeny-tiny does not mean it's any more appealing. Your child knows it's still a boring old meatball, doll-sized or not!

It wasn't the guest that was the problem, anyway, it was my mother. Every time she promotes one of her cook-books, I get trotted out like a specimen. She's talked about me in interviews. I've been in photos on the back of her book, looking enthusiastic while I pretended to eat something. I even had to be her sous chef the time our local TV station had her come on for their morning show and make her special soy blondies (aka her "SoLongy SoBlondies"— don't ask about the name, it's the worst).

Mom got so overly enthusiastic that while she was serving the blondies to the news anchor and the weather guy, she described them as "Amazeballs." Twice. I almost died. But instead I valiantly pretended I thought the whole thing was, yep, amazeballs!

This time, I didn't feel like pretending that having food allergies was so great. Let Jackson hang out with Dr. Mehta. He's the one who's obsessed with all things medical anyway, not me.

"I don't feel that well, actually," I said, trying to make a coughing noise. "Something is going around school. A virus. I better go lie down. And I have all that homework." I looked hopefully at Mom.

Mom gave me a not at all sympathetic look.

Of course she wasn't going to let me off the hook for her precious cookbook.

Great. Just great.

Chapter 9

Dinner was fine. But I couldn't bring myself to be the life of the party, or even polite.

After Jackson and I cleared the table, we were excused and I went to go sit in my giant beanbag chair and wait for my parents to come in to lecture me about my admittedly not-so-fabulous behavior. I felt too guilty and distracted to start on my homework. Instead, I turned up my music loud enough to drown out any footsteps coming down the hall and took a *Does He Like You Back or What?* quiz in a magazine I'd bought over the summer and forgotten about.

I thought about Ethan while I was answering each quiz question, like "What did he do on your birthday?" (Nada.) and "When's the last time he complimented you?" (Seven years ago, when he told me my Dora pj's were colorful.)

I added up my score. The quiz results said, "He's Intrigued."

That sounded like a big "denied" to me, because the other two results you could get could were, "He's So In Love" and "He Can't Get Enough of You." "Intrigued" was for sure the worst of the three. You'd think the magazine writer would have just admitted, "He's Kind of Meh on You so Maybe You Should Move On, *Loser*."

Intrigued, schmintrigued.

There wasn't a peep from either of my parents, not even after I saw Dr. Mehta's car drive off over an hour later.

At bedtime, I stepped out of my room to wash up as quietly as I could, hoping to get through the rest of the night without a lecture, but Mom was in the hallway. It was like she'd been waiting for me. Her hair was wet and she was in her fuzzy robe that has blue and pink cupcakes all over it.

"Do you feel like your behavior tonight was mature?" Mom said.

"Mom, I know! I'm sorry!" I yelled it though, which made me sound not as sorry as I should have sounded, even though she was right.

"When we have a guest here, I expect good manners." With that, Mom turned and went into her bedroom without waiting to hear what I had to say.

I went to bed feeling awful. And also, of course, hungry. That'll show me not to get up from the table before I'm full.

That off-my-game mood stayed with me for the whole next morning too. I pretty much moped, not walked, to school, ignoring Jackson as he went on and on *and on* about how awesome Dr. Mehta was.

As I was walking on the side pathway up to Woodgrove, I saw Jody getting dropped off by her dad. She mouthed, "WAIT!" and gestured at me to wait for her to get out of the car so we could walk in together.

"Are Brianna and Shelley having a huge party for the whole grade?" she asked as soon as she caught up to me. "That sounds so cool. Do you know who's going?" Jody flipped open the front pocket on her purple zebra print messenger bag and took out a lip gloss.

Her question totally took me by surprise. I had no clue Brianna and Shelley made their official party announcement. I wondered where Jody heard about it.

"I don't know," I admitted. "I guess, well, I don't know much about it."

"Actually, I overheard them talking about it. I figured you'd have more of the details."

"I'm not really hanging out as much with Brianna these days," I replied. "You know I'm...she's...everyone is so busy with everything." Even though it was noisy, with tons of other kids racing by us and yelling, it felt like the whole school must have heard me say that out loud.

"Oh." Jody looked at me and seemed curious but didn't say anything else. I was sure she was dying to ask me about Brianna, since of course she'd noticed what was going on, but didn't want to seem like the hugest gossip.

When we walked in, Brianna and Shelley were already there, talking to each other. They had on matching dark skinny jeans and fuzzy boots and hoodies, Shelley's a pure, snow white with not even a speck of dust or dirt on it; Brianna's was yellow. Their hair even matched—straight and shiny, each of them sporting a thin braid on one side of their heads. They'd both dyed a streak of their hair purple. They had taken time to coordinate outfits, like Brianna and I used to do.

They both looked really good.

Glancing down at my now-awkward-looking black capris and long-sleeved red tee, I felt less like a seventh grader, and more like my little cousin Beth who refuses to leave the house unless she matches her sparkly socks to her sparkly shirt and sparkly headband. I was definitely not by any stretch sophisticated. Or elegant.

"Do you want to go sit down?" I asked Jody, motioning to the bench near where Brianna and Shelley were sitting.

They looked both of us over as we got closer, and I saw Jody adjusting her shirt, tugging it down over her jeans, and flipping her hair back with her hand. Maybe she felt babyish too. Shelley and Brianna both said hi, but Brianna didn't shuffle over to make room for us to squeeze in next to her, so I stood awkwardly instead, watching the second hand on the big wall clock tick along until first period started, trying to focus on what Jody was saying instead of worrying about what I was missing.

Feeling so stupid and hanger-on-y was why when I got to the cafeteria for lunch later that same day, I'd already made myself a promise that I'd sit anywhere besides at Brianna and Shelley's table. Even eating alone was looking like a better alternative.

Almost.

When I got inside, I wasn't sure what my plan was, but then I saw Tiernan and everyone else at the peanut-free table. I walked over and stood there shyly until they noticed me.

"Yo, Nina." Tiernan slid his tray over to make room for me, and I sat down between him and Madison.

"Hey," I said. "Hi, Madison."

"Nina, wait, you're allergic to eggs, right? Hang on." Madison took out a wipe from her backpack and cleaned off the table where she'd been sitting. "Mayo," she explained. I noticed that each of her fingernails was painted in a different mega-bright Day-Glo color, which matched the rubber bands holding her braids.

"Oh, thanks. You didn't have to do that," I said, putting my brown bag down on the shiny, still-wet table. I was surprised. No one ever remembers what I'm allergic to in the first place, and the few that do wouldn't even realize mayonnaise has eggs. They're all like, "Oh, wait, you can't have this?" or "But I thought you couldn't drink milk," or "Can you eat chicken?" "Don't you wish you could have an omelet? That's sooooo sad that you can't."

It's annoying.

"I don't mind," she said. "Not a big deal."

"What's going on?" I asked, to no one person in particular.

"We're talking about doing something for the Halloween Talent Show," said Shane. "I say it would be cool. At my old school, everyone got into our talent show. It was huge, and there were judges there who worked at record labels and everything."

Heidi laughed and made a face. "That's New York City though. There's no way it's going to be a big deal here, Shane. Usually it's really small and a lot of people don't even go."

"So what?" Shane shrugged. "We could make it major."

Just then I heard a scream of "No way!" I turned to see Shelley giving Brianna a big hug—and they were both laughing super loud. My stomach felt funny again.

"We should start a band and name it The EpiPens," I said, turning away from Bri, acting like I didn't care about what she was doing or thinking. "I mean, half of us have to carry them around anyway. Might as well make a joke out of the stupid things."

Bringing my EpiPen with me everywhere I went was like having a stupid pimple that never went away! Besides, like I was going to have the guts to stab myself with a giant needle in the leg if I ate something I was allergic to anyway. Wouldn't I be too busy barfing or fainting or something else awful to be my own doctor?

"Dude, yes! Awesome idea!" Shane said, putting down his weird drink box so hard some of it splashed back out onto his retro band T-shirt. "Who's with us? Who here can play an instrument anyway?"

"Me," said Tiernan. "The guitar."

Madison was laughing. "Does the flute count?"

"Oh, you know it," said Shane. "Heidi, what can you play?"

"Nothing, really," said Heidi, picking at a slice of orange.

"That's not true," Tiernan said. "You have an awesome

voice. You're the only one in music class who can actually sing. Poor Mrs. Urbano probably wishes she had earplugs when she has to listen to the rest of us try to belt out 'Let It Be.'"

"That's not true," said Heidi.

"I swear, I have seen the giant Tylenol bottle she keeps tucked in her desk drawer for all those headaches she gets from our voices. But the point is that you have a great voice."

"Thanks," said Heidi, and amazingly, she smiled a huge happy smile at Tiernan. *Whoa, that was a first!*

Tiernan smiled back and rolled his hand in a little circle and did a mock bow over it, like something old-fashioned he'd seen in a movie that involved people who jousted.

"Nina, what can you play?" Shane already had a notebook out and was writing down all our names on it.

"The drums, but I'm not all that—"

"A girl drummer? Yes!" Shane pumped his hand. "That is money in the bank!"

"I'm not all that great," I finished.

"Who cares? Girl. Drummers. Rock. That's some serious cred."

"Cred with who, exactly?" said Madison, looking dubious.

"Everyone. Just ask anyone in the biz. Ladies on drums are *in*."

"Okay, guys, wait. I'm not so sure about this after all," I said, hunching over so my chin was almost level with the table.

"Why not?" said Tiernan. "Shane's right. It'll be fun. Why should the talent show blow anyway? Is there a town law that only the untalented must apply?"

"Come on, Nina, if I'm going to play the flute in front of the whole school I need moral support. At least you can hide behind your drums," Madison said.

"We could get T-shirts that say *The EpiPens* on them," said Shane. "We could write a song that's called 'The EpiPen Blues,' or maybe 'Anaphylaxis Anarchy.' Whoa, wait, whoa. Hang on. Listen. What if we got EpiPen to sponsor us and send us on tour?"

"Dude, dream on," said Tiernan.

"Yeah, let's actually practice first," said Heidi. "I doubt anyone is going to sponsor us, anyway."

"Except the ear plug company," I added. "Or the soundproofing people."

Shane ignored us both. "Okay, Heidi, vocals. Tiernan, guitar. Nina, drums. Flute courtesy of Madison. And yours truly on keyboard. I can ask my dad about us practicing in his studio too." Shane put his pen down.

"Your dad has his own studio? Where?" Madison asked.

"It's in our basement," Shane said. "He had it built when we moved up here so he wouldn't have to go back and forth to the city all the time for work. He's in the industry."

"What industry?" Heidi asked.

"What industry? *The* industry! Music. Obviously," Shane answered, surprise in his voice.

"I still have to think about it," I said. "I'm kind of rusty on the drums." What I didn't say to them was the truth: I wasn't sure if I was ready to be labeled as a complete and total dork, which is no doubt what would happen if we signed up for the talent show, or if I could truly handle everyone in the school—especially Shelley and Brianna—laughing at me if we bombed.

"H i, Nina," said Dad, not turning around. He was sitting on the couch typing on his laptop when I got
home that day.

"Hi, Dad." I gave him a wave and kept walking toward
the kitchen. Then I turned back again.

"Um, Dad?" I said, sitting down next to him.

"Mmm?" He sounded like he wasn't totally listening, which is what he does when he's in front of the
computer working.

"Remember how I used to play the drums?"

Dad turned to me when he heard that. Nothing gets
him to stop researching monarch butterflies, which is his
job, faster than talking about music. He's even in a cover
band with a few other people from the ecology department
at the college he teaches at. They call themselves Thin
Vitae, a name that for some reason cracks up every adult.
Me? Not so much.

Anyway, they "jam" (yes, seriously, that's what he calls

it) once a week to oldies music in their faculty lounge. They even play the annual student/teacher picnic. And Dad was so gung-ho that I share his love of music that when I was ten, he signed me up for two weeks of *Girls! Rock! Camp!* in New York City where Grandma lives. He convinced me to go, even though I was intimidated by the whole idea, but after the two weeks of being bossed around, big time, by a woman with long hair and a grumpy attitude and a series of faded T-shirts who said she played backup on a bunch of alt-country albums, I could at least keep a beat.

It was actually fun.

Dad was beyond ecstatic. I thought he was going to pass out when we had the concert for the parents on our last day and we played Metallica's "Enter Sandman." I think I saw him get teared up after the show when everyone was having juice in those tiny paper cups that always get all soggy. He made all the other professors he works with watch the video of my big drum debut and showed it to any college student unlucky enough to enter his office for months afterward.

Mortifying.

But I am actually okay on the drums, or at least I was when I was still playing. Not exactly good, and certainly not great. But I took lessons for a year after *Girls! Rock! Camp!*

and I can still keep the beat. But then Brianna kept saying that my drumming lessons and practices were cutting in to our time to hang out together and that drums were a "boring instrument," so I told my parents I was too busy with homework and I quit, even though I sort of didn't want to—I didn't think the drums were boring, and I knew Dad was bummed because he'd hoped I'd stick with it.

It had been way too long since I'd even seen a drumstick, let alone picked one up.

"Of course I remember you playing drums. 'Enter Sandman!'" Dad made a shredding air guitar move, almost knocking over his computer. Did I mention the part about him having a beard and how his hair is going gray? I'm not sure air guitar is really right for him anymore, not that I'd ever tell him that.

"Right, well, some friends and I were talking about maybe forming a band to play at the talent show."

"Hey, that sounds great. Anyone I know?"

"Um, I'm not sure. Well, I mean, you know Tiernan Albert."

Did Dad know anyone I went to school with other than Brianna? Had I even invited anyone else over since, like, third grade?

Ugh. Talk about depressing.

"I always had a band going when I was your age. I loved it," he said.

"You know, Shane, that's one of the guys who wants to do something for the talent show, he said girl drummers are cool."

"Women drummers *are* cool!" said Dad, super excited. "Meg White, Gina Schock, Moe Tucker."

"Isn't Moe a guy's name?"

"This is a female Moe. Also Karen Carpenter, Sheila E., Debbi Peterson, Janet Weiss. I'm sure there are more recent names that I won't know about because your old man is too old and out of the loop. What's that band you all like? The Neon Knickers? Don't they have a female on drums?"

Dad has a photographic memory. It's amazing. He can look at a map once and never need to see it again. Greatest skill ever.

He started typing something on his computer and pulled up an old-looking music video. He pointed at it. "See?" I sat down on the couch next to him and squinted. The outfits were kind of crazy, but the drummer was awesome.

"That's Sheila E.," he said, nodding his head along with the music.

"I kind of feel weird about being in a band," I said.

"Why? What's wrong with playing music? You like music, right?"

"Yeah, I know, but like, is it too showy?"

"Showy? I don't really know what you mean by that." Dad did look confused.

"I don't know. I just feel funny about it. Like I'm asking for attention." I shrugged. I couldn't quite even explain what I was feeling. Normally I just did stuff because Brianna was doing it and made me do it with her. I couldn't think of the last thing I decided to do on my own.

No wonder I felt like a turtle without a shell.

Dad nodded. "Well, it's always hard to start something new. You think about all the things that won't work. Or that could go wrong. But it's just music. If you don't like playing together, you can stop. Are these nice kids?"

"Yeah, they're totally nice, Dad. Actually, they're all the ones who sit at the peanut-free table in the cafeteria."

Dad didn't intend to hurt my feelings when he asked, "What about Brianna? Won't she be in the band too?"

But it did.

"She doesn't like me anymore, Dad." When I said "Dad," my voice broke, and I started crying.

"Hey, hey, don't cry, honey." He put the computer

down on the coffee table so he could pat me on the back, sort of awkwardly. "I'm sure that isn't true."

"No, it is." I rubbed my eyes. "She doesn't want to hang out with me at all anymore."

"What happened?"

"I don't know. It was the summer and she was in Italy and she saw Shelley there and now they're best friends or something, and they act like I'm just the loser who follows them around."

Dad didn't say a word.

"And she won't ever text me back and now they're planning a party together," I continued, still crying. "And they're calling it 'Sheliana's Massive Halloween Party.'"

"Oh. That sounds awful," he said, shaking his head back and forth, like someone died.

"It is!" I said.

"Sheliana is a thoroughly ridiculous name." He said it very seriously, but I knew he was teasing me.

I cracked up a little through my tears and drippy nose. "It is sort of stupid."

"I'm sorry, Nina. That sounds disappointing." He patted me on the shoulder. "Have you tried to talk to Brianna?"

"Dad! I did, like twenty times!"

"Okay, okay. Good for you for trying. Sometimes

things happen with friends and it's hard to know why. I know how much Brianna means to you."

"Not anymore," I said.

"I'm sure that's not the case."

"It is! I hate her." I rolled my eyes.

"Then go wail on the drums to get rid of all your righteous anger." Dad pretended to do a drum solo.

He is a goof, but it made me smile.

"Yeah, maybe you're right. I could try it once and if it's the worst ever, I don't have to go back."

"Would you need to bring your kit to rehearse? Where are you guys thinking about doing this, anyway? School?"

"No, that new kid, Shane McCormick, says his dad has a studio in their house. They just moved here."

"Wait, McCormick. Is his father Thomas McCormick? *The* Thomas McCormick?" Dad sounded all excited.

"Who?" I had no clue what he was talking about.

"Thomas McCormick. I heard a rumor that he moved up here this summer. He's quite a well-known indie record producer. That's incredible." Dad looked impressed.

"I don't know if that's Shane's dad. He said his dad had some music job. I'll ask, but I'm not even sure if anyone will remember that we talked about this by tomorrow."

They were probably all joking and they'll drop the ball and never mention it again.

I could hope, couldn't I?

Chapter 11

"Nina! Nina! Over here!" I heard my name being called the second I stepped in to the cafeteria the next day. I looked over to see Tiernan, Shane, Heidi, and Madison yelling and waving at me like it was some relay race and I was the person with the baton.

Not only could I hear them loud and clear, but so could everyone else in the building. As I walked past what felt like an endless row of tables, my head hanging low, I noticed Josh Ricci giving me one of his stupid smirks. I hate that guy. Mom always lectures, "Don't say 'hate,'" but you know, some people are just loathsome.

"Uh, hey," I said quietly, when I got over to where Tiernan and everyone were sitting, blushing from all the attention. I'm more of a blend-in kind of girl.

"We're talking about the talent show," Madison said. She held up a piece of paper with a sketch on it of a big silver needle and an arm with a drop of bright red blood flying out of it. Over the picture were the words "The EpiPens" written in messy-ish lettering.

"This is if we want to make up a poster to promote us," she continued. I forgot Madison was super artsy. Her mom, Leslie, teaches a lot of kids' classes at our local craft store on stuff like knitting and origami. I used to beg my mom to let me take them when I was younger. I don't really have the crafty gene though. When Leslie's classes were over, I'd have a tiny, sloppy, off-kilter bookmark to show for my efforts and in the same time Madison would have made a cool scarf and matching gloves that had the correct number of fingers.

"That's really impressive, Madison," I said. It was. The needle and the arm it was jabbing were really realistic and lifelike. It was hard to believe something that gross was drawn by the girl who wears rainbow-striped toe socks and the occasional pair of overalls to school.

I guess it's like my grandma says, "You never know about people."

Madison smiled at me. "Thanks!"

"It's not very, um, attractive, is it?" said Heidi.

"Rock isn't supposed to be pretty," said Shane, all seriously, like he was giving a lecture.

"Guys, it's all about the music," Tiernan said, wildly

waving his hands around, "AND THE MUSIC WILL BLOW THIS SCHOOL AWAY!!" The table next to us turned around in unison to stare. Heidi giggled.

It was unbelievable how gorgeous Heidi looked when she smiled. Maybe she wasn't pouty, just shy, because I hadn't caught her pouting once since I'd been sitting at her table. Also, she was, honestly, about a hundred times prettier than Shelley or any other girl I knew could ever be, but she didn't seem to care, or even realize it. Maybe all the years sitting in the wilderness of the peanut-free table warped Heidi's sense of reality.

"Can you guys come over after school tomorrow to practice?" Shane asked. "My dad said it's fine, we can hang out in the basement. He isn't having any bands over. I mean, other than us superstars, that is."

We all looked at each other.

"Sure," Tiernan said.

"Me too," Heidi smiled. A world record!

"I think so," Madison said. "I have to ask my mom because I'm supposed to help her teach her after-school beading class, but I bet she won't mind if I skip it."

Everyone turned to look at me.

I'd gotten amped about the band idea last night when I was with Dad. He'd gotten more gung-ho the longer we talked, and I couldn't stop him from going in to the garage and digging through piles of old bicycles and dingy lawn junk he's saving for a yard sale to get my equipment. He even helped me set it up in my bedroom and listened as I played—rustily—a few songs.

But now in the fluorescent cafeteria light of day, I was having a major internal debate: duck out before it could turn out to be a disaster, or go along with it because it was preferable to sitting home alone obsessing over my lack of a best friend?

"Uh," I said, hesitating. "I'm not sure. Sometimes I have to go home to babysit my brother." That was a lie. Jackson is allowed to be home alone in the afternoon by himself even after that time he turned on the oven to make Shrinky Dinks when no one else was around. My parents almost strangled him for that stunt. Too bad they didn't.

Shane looked at me blankly, blinking once.

"Actually," I added, in a big rush before I could stop myself, "I'm sure I can come too. Count me in."

"Awesome," Shane said. "Here, give me your cell phone." He reached his hand out. It was all freckly. I had been wondering why Shane looked familiar. It was because he looked like a kid who should star in a movie about a kid who is always getting into trouble. I handed him my phone.

He typed quickly without even looking at the screen, talking to us the whole time. "Here—that's my info. See you tomorrow."

The next morning, I was already seated in homeroom when Shelley, Brianna, and Josh walked in together. Ethan was a few feet behind them. When Shelley noticed he was there, she started giggling like crazy and leaned back to purposely bump right into Ethan's nicely tanned arm.

"Hey!" he yelled, rubbing his arm like it hurt, but he was smiling, not annoyed.

It reminded me of one of the questions from my love quiz: "If you casually touch him, how does he react?" It seemed like Ethan was more than just "intrigued" by Shelley. I didn't realize he was even friendly with her! *Gah!*

"A-HEM," said Mrs. Cook, staring at them. They took one look at her face and all raced for their seats, though I caught Shelley giving Ethan one last flirty look. Could she be any more obvious?

I felt really mad all of a sudden. Actually, not mad. Jealous. Of course the boy I thought was cute, the one I'd been thinking so much about, was the one Shelley liked too. Why couldn't I get a crush on any other boy in the entire seventh grade? Why couldn't *she* stop stealing all *my* people?

"Please look up to the bulletin board," Mrs. Cook said, pointing toward the sheet of light green paper hanging up. We all turned dutifully in that direction. "It's for the Halloween Talent Show. If you're interested in being a part of it, you have until October fifteenth to sign up." A few kids giggled, like it was some big joke.

Tiernan looked over at me and caught my eye. He lifted up his eyebrows, like he was asking a question. I put my face in my hands. Maybe this was a sign from the universe telling me something important about my life. I just wasn't sure exactly what.

Thanks for the help, universe. You're doing quite a job over here.

Chapter

12

Dad cheerfully—suspiciously cheerfully, if you ask me—drove me over to Shane's house that afternoon. I think he was secretly trying to sneak a peek at Mr. McCormick's studio. Jackson tagged along.

Shane's house was huge and looked like a fancy barn. It was far back off the main road, on a bumpy dirt road with pebbles that kept dinging and popping up on our car. When we got to the front door, a man with a really giant beard answered. He looked like a lumberjack—he even had a flannel shirt on.

"Hi," I said. "Is Shane home?"

"We're inside!" I heard Shane yell.

"Um, bye," I tried to duck inside but Dad tapped me on my shoulder.

"Hang on, honey," he said. He stuck out his hand. "I'm Dave Simmons. This is Nina, and my son Jackson."

"Thomas McCormick," said the lumberjack. "I'm Shane's father."

"Nina, why don't you go through here," Shane's dad pointed to his left. "Then down to our basement. Shane and your other friends are all downstairs already."

"Call me when you want me to pick you up!" Dad yelled as I walked off, then I heard him say, "So Nina says you just moved to the area."

Sigh. I hoped he wasn't going to try to talk to Shane's dad about his job, or please, please, no, invite him to one of Thin Vitae's shows.

I sped up, waving good-bye behind me without turning around, and followed the directions Shane's dad gave me. The room I walked through had wood floors and huge windows that went from the very top of the high ceiling almost to the very bottom of the wall. It was bright even with no lights turned on.

"Shane?" I yelled when I got to an open door.

"Here!" he called back.

I walked down super-thick carpeted stairs. On the walls were framed photos of record albums I'd never heard of with little black and white signs on them. Thomas McCormick's name was on all of them too. He seemed like a big deal, just like Dad had said.

Everyone else was already there. Tiernan, guitar strapped over his white turtleneck sweater; Madison, holding her flute and frowning; Heidi, sitting on the floor, her legs crossed, biting her fingernails; Shane, fiddling around with the knobs on a speaker. I sat down next to Heidi.

"How's it going?" I whispered to her.

"Fine. Except Madison's mad because Shane made fun of her idea of a flute solo."

"Bands don't do flute *solos!*" Shane said to Heidi while giving Madison a grumpy look.

"Why not? You can make any instrument sound rocky," Madison said back to him.

"*Rock-y?* Whatever." Shane turned to me. "Hey, Nina. Come check out the drum kit. It's my Dad's spare one."

I went over and sat down at the drums, picking up a pair of drumsticks on the floor. The drum heads were brand-new, and when I tried them out, the sound was crisp and sharp. I got excited in spite of myself.

"Hey, this is a great set, Shane!" I said. He gave me the Shane head nod in reply.

"Maybe we should practice something we all know, to get warmed up," Madison suggested.

"Like what?" Tiernan said. "We sang 'This Land Is Your Land' last year in music until it was coming out of our noses. Maybe that?"

"Uh, no," said Shane, shaking his head. "Pass. And never speak of that song in my presence again."

"'Smells Like Teen Spirit'?" said Madison. "I definitely know my way around that one."

"'When Doves Cry'?" I suggested. "'Rock Lobster'?" Madison looked at me like she had no idea what I was talking about.

"'Twist and Shout'?" said Heidi.

"Good one," said Tiernan. "A classic." We all nodded. And stood there. None of us did anything.

"Nina—count it off," Shane said.

"Oh, yeah, right," I said, half laughing, lifting up my sticks over my head. "I forgot about that. Okay, everybody." *Click-click-click-click.*

I'd had the fantasy in my head of us being incredible, of playing together as one from the get-go. Dad talks about bands that together were greater than any one of the individual members, who sounded destined to play only with each other.

The reality was nowhere close. We were…horrible. Ear-bruising. The only one of us who didn't sound flat-out crazy bad was Heidi, who managed, against impossible odds, to actually keep a tune. Sort of.

"Hold it!" yelled Madison after about a minute. "Hold on!"

We all stopped. I could hardly have been the only person there grateful that she put an end to our misery.

"Guys, that sucked!"

"We just started, Madison, calm down," said Shane, looking annoyed. "You can't expect to be tight in one afternoon."

"It's probably because we don't have a bassist," Tiernan said, wrestling to take his guitar off over his bulky sweater. His hair was wilder than usual, and his face was sweaty.

"Maybe you need to turn it up a notch, dude," Shane said to him.

"Why didn't I think of that? Yeah, that will solve all our problems." Tiernan sounded huffy.

"Calm down!" shouted Madison.

"YOU CALM DOWN!" Shane shouted back.

Uh-oh.

This wasn't good. I slunk lower behind the drums. Drummers are lucky that way. I hoped speakers or instruments weren't about to start flying around like how they do on those crazy Top 100 Band Meltdowns shows Dad makes me watch with him.

"Everyone be quiet," Heidi said. "Let's all relax." She twisted her lip and blew out a large gust of air. "Why don't we listen to some music first, before we play? To help inspire us."

"I don't think anything is going to help," Tiernan said unhappily.

Heidi patted him on the shoulder and gave him a smile. He didn't even cheer up then. Talk about clueless! Heidi looked a little embarrassed and yanked her hand away, and then pulled the sleeves of her red hoodie over her hands like mittens.

I felt bad for her. It's not like she was always walking around hugging and grabbing everyone all day long like it was no big deal.

"I'll listen to something," I said, trying to seem enthusiastic. "I could use a break from that, ahem, MAJOR, SUPER INTENSE drumming workout." I flexed my shoulders and pretended to rub my bicep, hoping to break the tension. Drummers are supposed to be the funny members of the band anyway. Like that Muppet drummer, Animal.

"Okay," Shane said. "Here." He hopped away from the keyboard and pulled open a giant shiny gold curtain that covered the whole back wall. I hadn't even realized there was anything behind it, but there were rows and rows *and rows* of records. "This is my dad's collection. Whatever you want, he's got."

"Whoa," I said. "My dad would so be freaking out right now."

We clustered around the shelves of records, alphabet-ized by band, each one covered with a plastic sleeve. Shane ran up the basement stairs two at a time, yelling, "Dad, do any rock bands have flute players?" as he got to the top.

Mr. McCormick appeared at the foot of the stairs—I could only see him from the knees down. "You mean do any bands have a flutist?"

"Dad, yes, flutist."

"Jethro Tull. I have some of their stuff down there. Go check out 'Thick as a Brick.'"

"Jethro who?" Madison whispered to me. She didn't seem mad anymore.

"Is that under J or T?" I said to no one in particular. "Wait. Is Jethro a person?"

Shane raced back down, jumping down the last four steps all at once. He started flipping through the records, looking for one. "Here we go," he said, lifting up a turn-table and putting the record on. I actually know what a turntable is, because my father still has one, but I don't know how to use it.

By now, Tiernan was sitting back down on the floor, and Heidi went over to sit next to him.

"I'm starving," Tiernan said. "Shane, do you have any-thing to eat?"

"You came to the wrong house, dude," Shane said. "I can eat, like, three things. One of which is lettuce. We've got nothing. Wait, that can't be right. Let me go check, there must be something here."

"I'll go with you," Tiernan said.

"Me too," Heidi got up.

"Let's all go," I said.

Shane led us into a huge kitchen with white tiled floors, and a giant refrigerator, and a big metallic oven that I know is super expensive because anytime we go to the mall, Mom parks by the entrance to the appliance section of the department store so she has an excuse to walk through it and drool over the stove.

"Shane, this is a cool house," I said.

"Thanks. The kitchen is kind of a joke, though, considering how little cooking we do. My dad gets takeout a lot, and I pretty much live on those gross protein drinks, so it's not like we use it all that much."

Shane opened up the refrigerator door. "Grapes?" he said, pulling out a bowl with a bunch of green and red grapes.

"Sure," Madison said, grabbing one.

"Shouldn't we rinse those first?" I said, then realized that I sounded like my mom. Sheesh, talk about pathetic. It didn't seem like anyone heard me, so I took an unwashed grape and tossed it into my mouth like I was all cool and laid-back.

Look at me, world! I laugh at your stupid food sanitation rules! Mwah ha ha!

Tiernan grabbed a bag of blue tortilla chips out of a cabinet. "Okay if we eat these, Shane?" he asked, sitting down on a stool at the big black and white marble island right in the middle of the kitchen—which had a second sink in it, because um, one sink isn't enough? Mom also dreams of having an island someday. A kitchen island, not a tropical beach island, that is.

"Can I look at that label, Tiernan?" I asked, reaching for the bag.

"Oh, yeah, Shane, you may not have heard, but a few of us are allergic to nuts," Tiernan said, cracking up.

"And eggs," I reminded him.

"I can eat these chips," said Shane, reaching into the bag too. "Trust me. There's nothing in these but corn and MSG. Bottoms up, Nina."

I almost never eat at anyone else's house, except when I used to go to Brianna's, since her mom kept snacks on hand that were okay for me to eat. I pretend I'm not hungry, but I'm actually too embarrassed to ask anyone what's in the food they offer me. When I was younger and had play-dates, my mom told all the other parents they could always serve me fresh fruit, so I have probably eaten my weight in watermelon, strawberries, and clementines over the years. *Boring.* The whole time I was secretly and silently drooling over their boxes of cookies and granola bars and that magic-looking chocolate concoction, Nutella.

But I didn't feel shy asking to see the label at Shane's house. It was, like, a huge relief. I took a handful of chips and took a big bite out of one. Maybe it was being able to eat without worrying, or actually not be ashamed to read a label, but they seemed like the best-tasting, crunchiest chips ever.

And just like that, without my even making a decision one way or the other, The EpiPens became a band, with me as a member.

We started hanging out after school a lot, except Fridays, when Heidi had ice skating lessons, and Wednesdays, when Madison was at advanced sewing class and also when Tiernan's mom made him go to a therapist—Tiernan called her "Dr. Obvious"—to talk about his parents' divorce.

Dad was right: being in a band was fun. It was like a built-in activity so you don't even have time to get bored with each other. The only bad part was coming up with a song all five of us could agree on performing at the talent show. That was an epic, many-days-long feud.

I told everyone I didn't care, which was true, and Heidi said she'd be up for anything too, but Shane, Tiernan, and Madison couldn't agree and wouldn't let it go. It was insanity.

I'd get all these texts from each of them with links and videos and everyone insisting their suggestions were the best. There was tons of arguing ("If we don't do this song, we're fools and deserve to be mocked and have rotten tomatoes thrown at us on stage!") and trash talking ("Anyone who can stand to listen to that song for more than ten seconds has craptastic taste.").

Finally, during one heated afternoon, Shane called in his dad.

"We need your help," he explained, following Mr. McCormick down the stairs to where we were all waiting.

"Yeah," Madison said. "We need a cool song that won't be too hard for us to learn."

"One that at least seven other people have heard of, Dad," Shane added.

"But not so overdone that everyone's already sick of it!" I jumped in.

"Fine, but if I choose a song for you, you have to swear on a stack of Ramones records that you'll trust me on this, even if you haven't heard of it before."

"Fine," Tiernan said.

Mr. McCormick walked toward his stacks of albums, rubbing absentmindedly at his beard.

He pulled one out and put it on the turntable, moving the needle and then pressing play. I caught a glimpse of a corny-looking guy on the cover.

Uh-oh. We'd promised to play this one, no matter what.

"It's called 'Cruel to be Kind,'" Mr. McCormick said.

Then he walked back up the stairs, shouting, "You'll thank me for this someday," over his shoulder.

But Shane's dad was right; it was such the perfect song. We listened to "Cruel to be Kind" three times in a row, all nodding along.

"We're all in agreement on this?" Shane asked.

Everyone nodded again.

"Cool, cool. I'll send everyone the sheet music later."

For the next week, I couldn't get the song, especially the awesome "Baby, you gotta be cruel to be kind" chorus out of my head. I sang it nonstop around the house and whenever I was stuck taking Pepper for her morning walk—where I had to pick up her poop with a plastic bag and pray that the high school kids wouldn't drive by me mid-scoop.

Shane's dad had also told us if we needed to do a second song, we should pick one from his new band, The Flax Seeds, which he said were about to "blow up."

Somehow I didn't think the audience would be begging for more.

*T*oday's *the field trip!* I thought to myself the second I opened my eyes. I didn't even need the alarm to wake up.

Our class was going to visit a small dairy farm two towns over. The farm kept winning awards for "freshest tasting milk" while trying to build their business against mega-farms that have tons of cows and way more money.

It's kind of embarrassing to admit, but I spent a lot of time getting dressed and doing my hair that morning, which makes me sound totally pathetic and not the sort of person who cares about the right things, like cows. But field trips are *exciting*. It's like a party but during the school day. A dairy farm might not have been my top choice for a group outing, but it still sounded cool. One year for our class trip, we went to a Broadway show in the city, and another time, to a museum about an hour away to draw still lifes. I was really proud of the fruit picture I made, but I guess my parents didn't think it was so great because they took it down off the refrigerator after only having it up for about three days. The photo of Jackson getting his yellow belt in karate stayed up for almost a year. Go figure.

I'd decided to wear my favorite black skinny jeans and my new gray sweater with a black peace sign on it. I'd actually been saving that sweater for the occasion, not wearing it even once since I found out about our trip, so it would seem special. And sneakers since Mrs. Cook said we'd be doing a lot of walking and would have to "watch where we stepped." I even shampooed twice and used a deep conditioner sample I'd gotten from a magazine, then blew dry my hair, which unfortunately made me all sweaty and hot before I'd even left the house.

"Where's your coat?" Mom asked as I was walking out the door with Jackson to school. "What if it's cold at the farm?"

"Nah, I don't need it," I said. "It's super nice out today."

"Don't you want to bring one just in case? I can run up and get it."

"Mom, the farm isn't any colder than our street. I'll be fine."

She gave me her "I'm not saying anything else but if you come home frozen I'll say 'I told you so' a million times" look.

"I made you cookies to bring along." She handed me a brown paper bag, neatly folded closed. Amazingly, she hadn't written my name on it. It took about three years of reminding her before she stopped putting my name with a heart around it in big, blocky letters on all my stuff.

I peered inside suspiciously.

"Good Day, Sunshine Cookies. And Pumpkin Snickerdoodles," she said.

"Whoa, Mom, there are a lot here." How totally dorky does it sound to say "Snickerdoodle" out loud?

"You can share them. I made extra."

"I'll take one!" Jackson grabbed for my bag and accidentally smacked me in the arm with his elbow.

I yanked away from him, and gave him a shove. "LET GO!"

Brothers are so annoying!

"Jackson, I sent you some with your lunch too," Mom said to him.

"Thanks, Mom," I said, putting the cookies in my backpack.

"You have your EpiPen, right?" she asked me.

"MOM!!!"

I knew it! She can never stop herself from reminding me.

"Honey, I'm just double checking." She gave me a look again, like she was the mad one. Why was she mad? I was the one who was being treated like an idiot.

"You don't have to ask if I packed it. I don't forget. I *never* forget."

Mom sighed. I sighed. Then I gave her a hug. Even if secretly I wanted something store-bought and artificially neon pink sometimes, it was nice of her to make me cookies. And her desserts were guaranteed to be yummy.

She kissed Jackson on the cheek and headed back in to the kitchen. "Have a fun time! Call anytime if you need me."

Need her for what? Milking a cow on the fly? Sometimes Mom acts like she's the expert on everything, but I know for sure she's clueless about farm animals.

In Mrs. Cook's classroom, everyone was freaking out and giggling and being all excited. No one was sitting down or putting away their homework or anything. I couldn't help but get excited too.

Field trip!

Josh was at his seat and Shelley and Brianna were sitting on the table on either side of him. I saw Josh out of the corner of my eye. He was looking all sneaky about something.

"Are you *sure* you can come with us today, Nina?" Josh said, when I walked past. "I mean, what if you touch the cows and get sick?"

"'Eek, help me, a cow! I'm dying!!'" He yelled in a fake squeaky voice.

That stung, I admit it, but what felt the worst was Brianna didn't say anything to defend me. She giggled instead.

Had she been the one to get him to make that joke? Don't cry. Don't cry, I told myself, giving my hand a pinch. I just stood there until Tiernan, who must have overheard them, jumped in.

"She's not allergic to dairy, genius. It's eggs. Since when do cows lay eggs? Or are you really that stupid?"

"I don't know what she can't eat," Josh said, shrugging. "Whatever. It's *all* freaky to—"

Tiernan didn't even let Josh finish talking. "You're such an idiot, Josh. I hope you're ready to repeat seventh grade."

Tiernan turned his back on them and started talking to me. I couldn't quite understand what he was saying because my face was hot and the noise in my ears was so loud—like the rushing of water—but I pretended to nod along and even managed to say "Uh-huh" a few times, swallowing hard over the lump in my throat, then blinking fast and hoping no tears would come out.

"Line up, everyone." Mrs. Cook clapped her hands together quickly. Everyone in the room picked up their bags and walked over, moving around to stand near the person they wanted to walk downstairs with.

"I'll catch up with you," I said to Tiernan, backing up over to the corner of the room. "I forgot one thing."

Actually, I wanted to grab a tissue from the box Mrs. Cook keeps in the corner near her other supplies. I hoped that no one would see that my eyes were kind of wet and wonder why.

"Line up! Now!" Mrs. Cook repeated, even though everyone was already doing it.

She walked by us. "Tiernan, you're in the front. Hold this." She handed Tiernan a clipboard and pencil.

"Everyone get behind Tiernan to walk downstairs and wait in the lobby. QUIET!" Mrs. Cook yelled as everyone started getting loud. The room got silent and people began filing out. I kept my back to everyone until I heard the door shut.

I bent over to toss my wadded up tissue in the trash, and I heard a voice behind me say, "Where are you?" It was Mrs. Cook, who was noisily opening and shutting some drawers in her desk, her silver bracelet jangling loudly.

"Um, what?" I asked.

"Oh, Nina, excuse me. I wasn't talking to you. I can't find my apple. And I'm starving. If I don't eat every two hours or so, I start to feel woozy."

I looked at her, confused. That seemed like a lot of food breaks for a grown-up.

"I'm pregnant," she said, seeing my expression. She pointed at her stomach, which now that she mentioned it, did look like there was a tiny lump thing underneath her flower-print blouse. I had no idea. Whoops.

"I am always hungry these days, and when I don't eat, watch out."

I wasn't quite sure if she was joking but I took her warning seriously.

"I have all these snacks in my bag." I felt a little shy offering my food to her, but she seemed pretty focused on finding that apple. And Mom did send a lot. Also I did not want to see Mrs. Cook lose it right before our trip.

Mrs. Cook perked up and stopped searching through her desk. "What sort of snacks?"

I handed her the brown bag. "Snickerdoodles. Pumpkin, I mean. No, I mean Pumpkin Snickerdoodles. And Good Day, Sunshine Cookies. My mom calls them that because they have a lot of stuff that's healthy for breakfast but in a cookie, so it's really not a cookie so much as a breakfast. I mean..."

By then Mrs. Cook was eating a Good Day, Sunshine cookie.

"Thank you," she said.

The door to the classroom banged open, and I jumped. It was Ethan. Mrs. Cook just kept eating.

"I'm late; did I miss the bus? Sorry!" Ethan looked all rumpled and cute, like maybe he'd overslept. He had a faded light blue button down shirt on, untucked, and jeans that had holes in the knees, but definitely because he wore them a lot, not because he bought them that way. His hair seemed a bit wavier and longer than even when I'd stared at him the day before.

"Normally I would be displeased at your late arrival, Mr. Chan, but I am far too busy enjoying this delicious cookie." She pointed to the bag on her desk. "Would you like one?"

Mrs. Cook gave him the "come here" sign with her hand. "Nina, you don't mind if Ethan has one, do you?"

"No, totally, I mean, my mom sent a ton, I could never eat all of these, and..." I stopped talking. Nothing I was saying was even a little bit interesting.

Ethan took a Pumpkin Snickerdoodle. I just hoped he wouldn't ask me what they were called. The shame of saying Snickerdoodle to him would have been too much for me.

"Hey, this is good," he said. "Thanks."

Mrs. Cook stood up and brushed a few crumbs off her shirt. "All right, you two, let's get going."

We got on the bus, and Mrs. Cook took her seat in the front row next to Mr. Spies, the science teacher. Ethan and I looked around. Every single seat was taken, except for the two seats directly across from the teachers. The bus driver hopped on and took her seat behind the wheel, loudly slamming the door shut behind her. Mrs. Cook gestured for us to sit down in the two free seats.

We looked at each other, shrugged, and sat. The bus smelled kind of weird, like from gas fumes or something. And the plastic seats were all cracked in spots and felt cold. It didn't matter to me though.

"Nina, hand that bag over here, please," Mrs. Cook said, as the bus got going. She hadn't been exaggerating about how hungry she was.

"I don't think I've been to a farm since I was a kid," I said to Ethan, trying to find something to talk about. I hadn't expected to sit with him—I'd been planning on sitting with some of The EpiPens, or maybe Jody. It was so surprising and exciting! I was still processing the fact that he was right up close next to me. I hoped he was psyched too, and not disappointed. I wished I'd practiced fascinating topics of conversation instead of worrying about blow-drying my hair.

"My grandparents own a farm in Vermont," Ethan

said. "They make maple syrup and sell it to local stores near them. I go every year during sugaring season to help."

"Really? No way, that's so cool," I said. "I love maple syrup. I guess everyone loves maple syrup, right?"

"Yeah, although sometimes when we're visiting them, I get kind of sick of it after a while."

"I bet! Like, how many pancakes can you eat?" He didn't say anything, so I added, "I can eat a lot of pancakes."

I imagined eating them with Ethan and laughing over each bite. Standing at the stove together, flipping them onto a plate like we were running a cute little café. Maybe when he and I got married, we'd go live on the maple tree farm and have pancakes every day for breakfast...

"Here you go, Nina," Mr. Spies handed me back my bag. He was holding two cookies in his other hand, with a third hanging halfway out of his mouth. He had a crumb on his chin. The bag felt a lot lighter.

"Can I have another one?" Ethan said.

"Sure!" I said, too cheerfully.

"Ethan, what are you eating?" Josh called out from a few rows back.

"SIT DOWN, MR. RICCI!" Mrs. Cook boomed back, not even turning around to look at Josh. I wondered how she could tell Josh was the one who said that, or how she knew that he was standing up. I smiled to myself. *Ha! You can't have a cookie, tiny jerk.*

"Remember how you used to scream 'MONKEY!' all the time?" I said to Ethan, after we had been quiet for a few minutes.

"What? No, come on." He started laughing. "I didn't do that."

"Really, don't you remember, in, like, first grade, any-time we lined up or went anywhere, you were all 'monkey, monkey, monkey.' And you'd get in trouble?"

Because I'm not totally crazy, I didn't admit to Ethan that I'd been thinking about him a lot lately, and I even went back to look at some class photos from past years that I'd shoved into a box on my bookshelf. When I saw our first grade picture, with him wearing his monkey T-shirt, a goofy grin on his face, it made me remember how when he'd see a photo of a monkey in a book, he'd get all excited and then he started making up words that had monkey in them. Like if we were reading about elephants, he'd yell, "Ele-monk," or if we were doing math, and the answer was three, he'd scream, "THREE MONKEYS!" He got in trouble a lot. Ethan grew out of that phase a long time ago though.

"*Monkey!*" he whispered in my ear, and I cracked up. His arm kept brushing against mine, and every time the bus ran over a pothole, our knees or feet or legs would bump. I noticed that he didn't try to move away or act freaked out when we accidentally touched. The only bad thing about the whole ride was that it ended way too fast, and then everyone piled off the bus, and Shelley and Brianna and Josh caught up with Ethan, and he didn't look back once to find me after that. It made all the cool stuff we saw at the farm a little less cool, and I spent half the time trying to eavesdrop on what Ethan was talking about and missed the whole discussion about how cows give birth. I hoped that wouldn't be on the next science quiz.

Because I was so distracted, what happened next isn't that surprising. But understanding why doesn't make it any less awful.

So the farm owner, who said to call him Doug, was a former doctor who quit his medical practice to work on the farm. He looked old and dusty—the way I always think of farmers—and wore beat-up, worn-in jeans and heavy boots.

Doug was telling us about how important dairy is, and how on those giant farms there are too many cows, so the animals can't walk around in the fresh air or even get grass to eat, and they get injected with tons of medicine every day, whether they're sick or not. It sounded sad. And unappetizing.

Then Doug took us all back to the little farm stand that he and his family set up right by the side of the road so he could sell fresh milk to people driving by. His wife was there too, and their super cute college-aged son who was working behind the counter. He began doling out a sample-sized scoop of ice cream for all of us that Mrs. Doug, or whatever her name was, said was made right there on the premises.

Here's the thing: I always eat ice cream at home—like all the time, it's not a big deal. I don't usually eat it when they serve it at parties because without fail, it seems like the only flavor being offered is Peanutty Whipple Deluxe or something, with big chunks of nuttiness, but Farmer Doug said this was pure, straight-up, "classic" vanilla.

I'd seen Tiernan say, "No, thank you," when they offered him a sample. But Doug's son was adorable and I felt dumb about saying no to him, so I didn't. I just said, "Thanks," and took my cup. I wasn't going to have any, but it was just plain, creamy white—there was not a peanut in sight. It looked delicious. I saw everyone else digging in, and saying "Mmmm" and raving about how awesome it tasted and how they'd never buy ice cream from anywhere else again.

The thought of throwing the cup away, untasted, and having to go eat another dry, crumbly cookie instead seemed beyond depressing to me.

I hadn't seen one chicken on our tour, so I felt pretty confident there were no eggs in the ice cream. I mean, why call it a "dairy farm" if it was a "chicken and cow" farm?

I was bummed out thinking about Ethan and Shelley and whether he was into her.

But really it was just that I was so sick of missing out on the all the fun.

So I took a bite.

And then another one.

The ice cream was just as cold, creamy, sweet, and delicious as everyone was saying. I couldn't believe I'd almost passed it up out of fear.

As I was digging in for a third time, I realized something wasn't right about this ice cream. Because my throat felt itchy. And my lips started tingling.

I didn't move for a minute, hoping the feeling would go away, but it didn't. I pushed up the sleeve of my sweater, my hands shaking from pure, total terror, and I could see red welts appearing—growing larger and then disappearing, like some alien was invading my body and trying to burst free from my skin.

I yanked my sleeve back down and started running—away from my class and everyone, looking for a bathroom, or anywhere else where I could be alone and feel sick by myself, instead of in front of every single kid I knew.

I thought I heard someone call my name, but I didn't turn around. I had my bag with me. If I could make it someplace private, I knew I could use my EpiPen on myself. I'd never done it before, stabbed myself in the leg with a needle, but I had to do it now.

Hurry, I thought to myself. *Hurry hurry hurry.*

I didn't see a bathroom anywhere, and I was starting to feel dizzy and hot, so I sat down behind the barn where we'd had our tour. I unzipped my backpack and pulled out my EpiPen, but my hands were shaking so much I couldn't seem to uncap it. The Epi dropped to the dirt softly.

It was hard to take a breath—I heard gasping and realized it was coming from me.

Oh, no. Oh, no.

And then I heard a boy's voice say, "Nina? Wait, I'm getting Mrs. Cook," and then I can't remember what happened next, but suddenly I heard more people yelling and a lot of footsteps in the dirt and I think Tiernan telling someone, "She's got food allergies!" and Farmer Doug was sticking a needle into my leg and putting his hand on his wife's arm, looking her in the eye, and telling her very calmly, "Call 9-1-1."

Then, in what felt like only a few seconds, I could breathe again. I took a gulp of air. My hands were shaking so much I had to squeeze them together in front of me to try to get them to stop.

"I feel sick," I said, looking up at Farmer Doug. I realized Mrs. Cook was down on the muddy ground next to me, patting my back. She smelled lemony and her earrings made a quiet little jingling noise when she moved her head.

Doug stood up, rubbing his hands on his jeans. "It's the epinephrine. It makes you feel jittery. Some people throw up."

That got my attention. Everyone in my class was already staring at me. I couldn't imagine the deafening screams of horror if I hurled in front of all of them.

"Move, everyone, let's move it along," Mr. Spies said, guiding people away. "Let's give Nina some space."

I stared down at the ground, hearing people whispering, "Is she all right?" and "Oh my god, I totally thought she was going to die," and "What's wrong with her?" but I refused to look at them. My lips felt weird. I went to touch them, and my hand reached them before I expected it to. They were bigger than normal—they must have totally swollen up.

I heard a siren and looked to see an ambulance coming up the road. I slunk lower against the firm wall of the barn, appreciating the sensation of the wood digging into my back. Farmer Doug walked over to talk to the woman who got out of the ambulance driver's seat. Then he motioned over in my direction. Another person had hopped out of the passenger side of the ambulance and grabbed a stretcher from the back. Then they both came jogging up to me.

"I'm fine!" I said to them as they approached. They

ignored me, strapping a band around my upper arm to take my blood pressure. They listened to my heart. Finally they popped the stretcher open and lowered it so it was almost at ground level.

"I can walk," I insisted. This was getting more mortifying by the second. Maybe I'd fall backward into some cow dung for the ultimate indignity. I wondered if I could offer to work at the farm in exchange for living there so I'd never have to go back to school again.

"It's okay, Nina," said Mrs. Cook, more kindly than I'd ever heard her speak before.

I put my still-shaking hand on my forehand and took a deep breath, grateful and surprised to find air still coming in so easily.

I'd never take breathing for granted again.

The EMTs counted, "One, two, three," and lifted me on to the stretcher, strapped me in, put a blanket over my legs, and pushed me past the gawking faces of my entire class and into the ambulance. When the doors finally shut, Mrs. Cook still by my side, I threw up all over the blanket.

"What's a little vomit between friends?" the guy EMT said cheerfully, whisking the gray, scratchy cover off me.

"Is she all right?" Mrs. Cook looked worried.

He was taking my blood pressure and waited a second before replying.

"She appears to be. Are you having any breathing difficulties?" he asked me.

"No, actually, that made me feel better," I admitted. I hate throwing up. It's so hideous. I once heard a comedian make a joke about how barf always looks like someone had eaten peas and carrots, which is so true. Yuck.

"What day is it?" the EMT asked me, shining a small flashlight in my eyes.

"Wednesday. Really, I'm fine."

I guess I thought when I got to the hospital, twenty young and attractive doctors and nurses would rush out to treat me, and there'd be all this screaming and doors being flung open, like on TV, but when the EMTs wheeled me into the emergency room, they unstrapped me, lifted me off the stretcher, and stuck me on a bench in a busy hallway. No one looked that attractive, and one doctor even had a mustard stain on his dingy-looking white coat.

"Wait here," the first EMT said to me, like I really had anywhere else to go.

Mrs. Cook followed her to the front desk, where they started talking to someone behind the desk. Then Mrs. Cook came back with a nurse, and they escorted me to a bed in another room where there were other people on beds with thin light blue curtains half pulled around them for the bare minimum of privacy.

"How are you feeling now? Okay?" Mrs. Cook asked, once I was settled in and the nurse had checked all the same stuff the EMTs had just done earlier. "Your mother is on her way."

Mom! She was going to be furious. I felt like throwing up again.

Mrs. Cook must have seen my face, because she tried to distract me by talking about her cat. She took out her wallet to show me a picture of him.

"Here he is; this is Ghost."

"He's cute," I said, trying to be polite. I closed my eyes.

"You must be tired," Mrs. Cook said.

That was the last thing I heard before falling asleep, waking up when I heard my mother say, "Nina." She was standing right by my side and leaned over to give me a too-hard hug.

I started to cry. "Hi, Mom."

"What happened?" She was looking at my face with a worried expression.

"I ate some ice cream. I'm so sorry. It had eggs, I guess. Unless there was a nut in there, but I don't think so." I was still crying.

"It's okay, honey. It's okay."

"It was vanilla, we always have that at home, and they said they make their own ice cream…"

"The school is so sorry, Mrs. Simmons," Mrs. Cook said. "I wasn't aware of Nina's allergies. I try to be on top of these things, truly."

"It's not your fault," Mom said.

She was right.

It was totally mine.

"Can we go home?" I asked, pulling on my mother's sleeve like a little kid. "I just want to go to bed."

"No, we have to stay here for a full four hours. They need to watch you and make sure you don't suffer a second anaphylactic attack."

Four hours. Miserable and smelling of barf.

For a second, it looked like Mom was going to cry herself, but she rubbed her eyes and took a deep breath. She stood up and faced Mrs. Cook.

"We're fine here. Thank you so much for making sure Nina got the medical attention she needed. Can I call you a cab?"

"No, it's quite all right," Mrs. Cook said, shaking Mom's hand. "I've already called my husband, and he said he'll come and get me when I'm ready. Please don't worry about me, just take care of yourself." Mrs. Cook gave me a hug. She must have been scared too. I felt bad, freaking out a pregnant woman.

Mom sat down on the foot of the bed and picked up the phone next to it.

"Dave? Yes, she's here. She's fine. Absolutely fine. Don't worry. Hang on, let me ask her."

Mom turned to me. "Do you want Dad and Jackson to come and keep us company?"

I shook my head no. Making a family party out of my awful day didn't seem like such a great idea.

After she hung up, she just stared at me.

"What?" I said. "What are you looking at?"

She took a loud, deep breath. The "I am going to kill you" breath she takes, like the time I shoved Jackson down half a flight of stairs and she sent me to my room for about eighty hours so she could cool down.

"What were you thinking? You could have died!"

"I know, Mom. I totally blew it."

"I was so terrified when they called me and told me you were being taken to the hospital."

Way to make me feel more awful.

"Mom, I know. I know."

Then Mom was crying. "I hate these damn allergies. I just hate them."

That wasn't the way she normally talked about them. Usually Mom is always like, "It is frustrating, but it's not the end of the world."

"They're not your allergies, Mom. They're mine. I'm the one who gets to hate them. *You* can eat anything! Dad can eat anything! Jackson can eat anything!"

"You think I like worrying about you every time we go out to a restaurant? Or get on an airplane? Or you go to a slumber party?"

A nurse came over and started talking my blood pressure again. Neither Mom nor I said anything until she jotted something down on a folder on the foot of my bed and walked away.

"If you hate my stupid allergies so much, why don't you stop writing your cookbooks?" I asked.

Mom wasn't crying anymore, even though her nose was red and dripping. She grabbed a tissue out of her purse and blew it.

"I write them so people know how to cook for you, and kids like you. I write them so I have an excuse to make you treats and keep you safe. And though I realize it sounds like a greeting card, I write them because when life gives you lemons, you make lemonade."

I rolled my eyes.

Lemonade my butt.

"Well, that's weird, Mom. I didn't ask you to do that."

Mom sighed. She didn't say anything for a while. I felt angry and guilty at the same time.

"Mrs. Cook liked your Pumpkin Snickerdoodles," I said, after the silence started to freak me out.

Mom smiled at me and blew her nose.

"I'm glad," she said.

"I really am sorry." I gave her a hug. She squeezed me back super tight.

"Nina, I'm just so relieved that you're okay. That's my only concern right now."

The rest of our time at the hospital was boring. There wasn't any of the drama like on medical shows with doctors making out in closets or crying to each other about love, or patients coming in with, like, a tree limb coming out of their kneecap. Mostly everyone seemed busy doing their jobs.

Finally, after hours of waiting and doing nothing, we finally got the okay to leave. I had a huge headache and couldn't wait to crawl into bed.

On the car ride, I checked my phone, which I hadn't been allowed to use because of hospital rules. I had, like, a million texts from everyone asking if I was okay. I checked first to see if Brianna was one of them. Amazingly, she was. She'd written, "I hope u r feeling better." I was shocked. She probably just felt guilty for being so mean before. Or maybe her mom made her do it. I was pleased anyway. It almost made me feel like the whole experience had been worth it if she was going to be nice to me again.

Almost.

The EpiPens all messaged me, and Madison even sent me a picture of herself holding up a sign that said, "Get Well Soon!" Jody and some other kids wrote too.

The phone rang as I was texting Brianna back.

"Hello?" I said.

"Um, Nina, hey, this is Ethan."

"Ethan?" My voice sounded squeaky.

"Yeah, I called before but your phone was off. I tried a few times."

"You called me before?" Wow, I was sounding super smart here.

"I wanted to, you know, see if you were okay."

"Oh, I'm fine. Totally. I'm already on my way home."

"Oh." Then he was quiet for a minute. "I'm glad. Your face was all blown up. I wasn't sure."

My stomach contracted. I must have looked disgusting at the farm. He was just calling because he felt sorry for me, and because he's the nicest guy and he hasn't even realized how cute and popular he is. He wasn't calling because he liked me. Who could like someone who was so weird and couldn't even have a bite of ice cream, especially when there were so many other normal, not puffy girls into him?

"I guess I'd better go," I said hurriedly. "Thanks for calling."

"Well, okay, I'll…" I hung up on him before he could finish his sentence.

"Who was that?" Mom asked me.

"Ethan."

"Ethan who?"

"Ethan Chan. You know, remember him?"

"Oh, of course! You haven't mentioned him in a long time. Monkey boy. Eep, eep." She was staring at the road, so I couldn't see her face.

"He's not into monkeys anymore."

"That was sweet that he called to see if you were okay."

"Mom, he just felt sorry for me. Everyone probably thinks I'm some huge loser."

"Nina, *no one* thinks you're a loser for having food allergies." She braked at a light and looked at me, sounding both concerned and annoyed at the same time.

"Well, *I* think I'm a loser for having food allergies."

"You're being very silly." She put her foot down on the gas pedal hard enough that we both lurched forward in our seats.

"Nice, Mom. That really felt great on my stomach. Don't get mad if I throw up all over the car. Anyway, whatever. You weren't there today at the farm, you didn't see how people were staring at me, totally disgusted."

"Oh, well, thank you for clarifying things for me. That Ethan sure is a jerk for calling."

Sarcasm again.

"Okay, Mom, I got the point, thanks."

"What other horrible people are checking in to see if you're okay? Those monsters!"

I giggled, but quietly so she wouldn't hear. I didn't want to give her the satisfaction.

Chapter

15

I vaguely remember getting home and my dad giving me a huge hug and Jackson staring at me and looking not at all jealous of my brush with death, just worried, and Mom helping me get into a T-shirt to sleep in, and being too tired to brush my teeth but doing it anyway because I felt so gross. I must have been out by the time my head hit the pillow, because that's the last thing I remembered until my alarm went off the next morning, more than fourteen hours later.

The worst feeling in the world is waking up happy and then realizing there's a reason not to be. It took me only a few seconds to get that awful "Wham!" punched-in-the-stomach feeling. I leapt out of bed and raced to the mirror, fearing the worst—but my face wasn't puffy or swollen or anything. I looked like myself, except I had dark circles under my eyes that were noticeable. That was weird for someone who'd just slept as much as I did.

I heard my parents talking in the hallway, and I jumped back under my dotted comforter.

No way was I going to school. Not a chance.

There was a knock and then the door was opening.

"Uh, yeah, come in?" I said. "I think I'm supposed to say that first, though, before you stroll in and make yourself comfortable."

"Very funny, honey," Mom said distractedly, holding her coffee mug in one hand. She was wearing her blue robe with the white fluffy clouds on it. She has a lot of bathrobes and aprons because we all buy them for her birthdays and stuff. For a while we got her a lot of coffee mugs, but last year she banned them, saying she was "all mugged out."

"Time to get up," she said cheerfully.

"What?! No. I can't go to school today. It'll be the worst dealing with everyone!"

"Well, you're perfectly fine. The doctor said there was no reason to stay home. Therefore, time to get going." Mom came and stood by the foot of my bed, absentmindedly smoothing out a crease in my comforter.

"No."

"Yes, Nina. I know yesterday was terrible, but now it's time to get back on the horse. Maybe going to school will take your mind off of things."

"I doubt it. I bet *some people* won't even care if I'm okay."

I crossed my arms over my chest and shot her my best attempt at the dramatic look I've practiced in the mirror.

She looked closely at my face then sat down next to me, smushing my leg a bit. "Listen, is someone bullying you?"

I wondered how to answer that.

"No, Mom, no bullying. Relax. Forget I mentioned it. I'm getting up."

"Are you sure? Really?"

"Yes, really. There are just a few total jerks, like there always are. But no bullying."

Mom waited a minute to see if I'd blurt out some big revealing detail. I wasn't afraid of anyone hurting me or anything like that. Just my feelings. What do you call it when your best friend excludes you from her life? It's not being bullied; it's being abandoned.

Even though I really, really didn't want to go to school, Mom was sort of right like she is more than I like to admit.

It was pretty clear I was going to have to return at some point, so getting the awfulness over with was probably the best move.

Like ripping off a Band-Aid.

Mom offered to drive me to school, and I kept dragging my feet and pretending I needed to do "just one more thing," so by the time I got to Woodgrove's lobby, just about everyone had gone in for first period. I took a deep breath and headed upstairs. When I stepped into the classroom, it got insane, pin-drop quiet. Like the silence right after someone drops their tray in the cafeteria before everyone starts laughing and clapping.

I had hoped everyone would have forgotten about the stupid ice cream incident, but who was I kidding? When the Segal twins, Duncan and Dominick, got a stomach bug last year and threw up at almost the exact same time in the cafeteria, people talked about that for a month. Almost dying and having my face blow up like a balloon was, like, sure to be the news of the decade. I just hoped no one was fast enough yesterday to have gotten a photo of me in all my glory, or if they did, they'd be open to bribes to delete it forever.

Mrs. Cook smiled at me, a friendly smile. After saying, "Good morning, Nina," she took attendance right away. I could tell there were a lot of people looking at me because, yes, I was freak-show girl, but at least no one said anything.

One time my mom and dad hired a local college student to come babysit us because they were going to be out at Dad's annual Biology Department Tofu 'n' BBQ Party—yeah, that's really the name. The cool thing was that Lisa the Drama Major showed up wearing silver high heels and she let me walk around the house in them. I was taller than I'll probably ever be again in my lifetime. I felt so elegant. The bad thing was that she also let me stay up late and watch this famous old horror movie *Psycho*, which was a lot scarier than I thought it was going to be. It was awful. I sat on the couch next to Lisa and bit my nails throughout the whole thing. My parents never let Lisa babysit for us again, and I had to sleep with my light on for the next three months.

The way I felt while I was watching *Psycho* was the way I felt sitting in Mrs. Cook's class right then. Waiting for something horrible to happen. I wished I could cover my face with a couch pillow like I had during the movie.

A few minutes before the period ended, I shoved all my stuff into my bag and slid halfway out of my seat. I was ready to bolt as soon the bell rang, hopefully avoiding speaking to anyone.

But it's not like I could magically teleport out of the classroom, and if someone wants to talk to you, they will find a way. Tiernan yelled, "Nina, wait!" the instant the bell rang, before I'd even made my move toward the door.

Wonderful.

I waited for him, blushing and doing everything to avoid meeting the eyes of kids walking by us. "What's up, Tiernan?"

"Um, oh, nothing, I had a cinnamon raisin bagel for breakfast, and my grandmother is coming over for dinner, and oh, yeah, you almost kicked the bucket yesterday. Otherwise, nothing much."

"Look, I'm totally okay. I just feel stupid. I'm hoping everyone is going to forget about what happened."

"Good luck with that. You're the talk of the school. Someone started a rumor you were in a coma."

"A coma!" I yelled. Two sixth graders stared at us and then whispered as Tiernan and I walked through the hallway together.

"Yep. Coma city. And another person told everyone they're second cousins with the ambulance guy, and that you made out with him on the ride to the hospital."

"WHAT?" I stopped short, which caused some kid behind me to step on my left ballet flat and scratch my ankle.

"Okay, I just made that one up." Tiernan started laughing. "I'm glad you're not sick. We were worried."

"We who?"

"Heidi. We hung out last night." Then Tiernan was the one blushing. "She came over to study."

"Uh-huh," I said, smirking.

"No, seriously." Tiernan looked annoyed. Good. Now there were two of us.

"It's okay, I believe you. Sure. Everyone loves *studying* together." I used my fake voice. Like I'd fall for the old "we were only studying" line..

"Anyway, I'll see you at lunch. We can talk about more interesting things," Tiernan said, trying to change the topic in such an obvious way.

"More interesting than your love life?" I couldn't help giving him another smirky face.

"I don't have a love life!" he said, loud enough for people to overhear. "Wait, I didn't mean that like it sounded."

"You sounded very smooth, Tiernan. The height of cool. In fact, Woodgrove Middle School should give you a special King of Cool award."

"Listen, just because you survived a near-death experience does not mean I won't smack you," he said, bopping me on my hip with his backpack then running off before I could get him back.

I should have known my brilliant plan to avoid everyone by wishing them away wasn't going to work. Here's how my day went:

Person: "Oh my GOD, Nina, are you okay?"

Me: "Yes, I'm fine."

Person: "I thought you were dead."

Me: "Nope, it's not a big deal."

Person: "I can't believe it. I would hate to have food allergies."

Me: "Well, yeah, they're annoying, but it's not the end of the world."

Person: "I feel SOOOOOOOOOOOOOO sorry for you."

Me: "Um, thanks. I guess."

Person: "Wait. Can you eat sushi?"

It was the longest morning of my life, so I was really looking forward to sitting with everyone at the peanut-free table and talking about music instead of my blowfish lips.

"Guys, tomorrow we can't practice at my place," Shane said at lunch, after everyone gave me big hugs and asked me if I was okay, like, eighteen times.

Shane took a big swallow of his lemon-lime drink box and then made a disgusted face and shook his head. He continued, "My dad's got a new band he's thinking about working with, and they're going to be using the studio, so we'll have to skip it."

"Shouldn't we try for one final practice?" Heidi asked, chewing on her fingernail and fiddling with the sleeve of her gray sweatshirt. "I'm gone the first half of next week for my cousin's christening in Chicago, remember?"

"Yeah, it's our last time together for six days," Tiernan

said. "Six days! What will we do without you, Heidi?" he pretended to cry, putting his head down on the table and making loud fake sobbing noises. He clutched at her hand. Heidi giggled.

"Oh, hey, what about my place instead?" Tiernan asked, lifting up his head and drying his pretend tears.

"What would we practice on?" Madison said. "I mean, I could bring my flute, but drums aren't portable."

"I'll pack up my drum kit," I said. "It's no problem."

"That sounds great," Heidi said. She gave Tiernan a cute, smiley look.

"Sure, if someone can give me a ride I can go," Shane said, pulling out his cell phone to type something. "Then I can bring my keyboard. Do you have an amp, Tiernan?"

"My mom can give you a ride," I said to Shane. "I don't think she'd mind."

Mind? She'd been asking me about the band and practice so much, I bet she'd be excited to get in the car with Shane and finally meet him. Hopefully she wouldn't overdo it with the enthusiasm and ask if the band sounded "amazeballs."

"Done, and done," Tiernan said. "Yes, we have amps. I'll give my mom a heads-up and warn the neighbors the rock stars are arriving. Roll out the red carpet!"

Mom was excited when I told her we'd be going to pick up Shane. She actually turned off her hand mixer to discuss the details with me.

"Mom, there's not much to talk about. I'll come home from school, I'll put my drums in the car, we'll go pick up Shane, and then you can drive us both to Tiernan's mom's house. Okay?"

"That sounds great!" she said.

"Or I can do it," Dad volunteered, looking up from his computer.

"No, it's not a problem. I can make time to give Nina and her friend a ride. I'm happy to." Mom beamed at me like I'd given her a huge present.

I rolled my eyes. It was just a car ride. We drive all the time. But I guess parents don't have much else to look forward to, and Mom is not the calm type when it comes to meeting my friends. Other parents are all, "Oh, who are you again?" when their kid's friends come over, and let them watch TV or play video games all day.

Mom, on the other hand, offered to pack up some cookies she "just happened to have baked" in case my friends wanted a snack, so I had to explain about how

Shane was allergic to all foods except lettuce and corn and unless she had a plan to make a cookie using only those two ingredients, we'd have to skip the food portion of the day. She took it fairly well. She only asked, "Are you sure that's all he can eat?" three times.

"I want to say hello to Shane's father," Mom said, as we turned on to Shane's street.

"Mom, no! He has a band over and they're busy recording or rehearsing or something. *Please* just stay in the car."

Shane must have seen us drive up, because he came out of the front door as we were pulling into his driveway. He was wrestling slightly with his keyboard.

Shane put his equipment in the back of our car and walked around to sit next to me in the seat behind Mom.

"Hi," Mom said, turning around to smile.

Shane reached forward to shake Mom's hand. "Nice to meet you," he said.

"Ready to rock?" Shane said to me, sliding his cell phone into his long-sleeved T-shirt pocket.

"Ready," I said.

"How's the band?" Mom asked, talking extra loud from the front seat so she wouldn't have to turn around. *Groan.*

"My dad says we sound really tight," Shane said, leaning

forward a little against his seat belt, explaining his plans for us to break out. Shane will talk to *anyone* about music.

It wasn't long before I saw Tiernan's house. Made it!

"Call when you're ready to get picked up," Mom said, waving cheerfully to us as she pulled away.

Practicing at Tiernan's was pretty much the identical experience as at Shane's place. We spent the first half hour talking about our day and complaining about homework and our teachers and whatever else we felt like. Then those of us who can eat actual food had a snack. Everyone made a big deal out of my not having something I'm allergic to. Like I'd *ever* do anything that stupid again.

Finally, when we'd killed all the time we possibly could, we got ready to play. It was sort of tricky though, because Tiernan doesn't have a rug on his bedroom floor, so the drums kept sliding away from me and I had to concentrate extra hard to keep them from jamming into the back of Heidi's legs while she was singing.

Between trying to avoid kicking the kick pedal too hard and counting under my breath to keep up with the music, I was too busy to notice until halfway through the song that Ethan had come into the room. He was standing by the door to Tiernan's bedroom, holding a video game.

Talk about startling! And because I can't get surprised

without making a total idiot of myself, I lost the tempo and slowed way, way down. Heidi turned to look at me, with a "What the…?" face. I blushed, big time.

"Dude!" Tiernan said, as the rest of the band stopped playing. "It's already six o'clock?" He gave Ethan a high-five. "I didn't realize we'd been practicing for so long."

"Hey, that was cool. You guys were good," Ethan said, sounding like he meant it.

"We're awesome, right?" Shane nodded at Ethan from behind the keyboards.

"Hey, Nina," Ethan said to me, running one hand through his hair. "How are you feeling?"

"I'm fine," I mumbled.

"Tiernan told me you were all in a band together," Ethan said, looking at me, not anyone else.

I shrugged.

Heidi turned to ask Tiernan a question, and Shane and Madison leaned in to hear what they were saying. Ethan stood there for a minute. I had so many things I wanted to say to him—funny, smart things, the kind of stuff I always think of when I'm alone in my room, pretending I've been cast in a movie as a gorgeous wild-child who everyone is always in love with and who wears dangly earrings and I'm being interviewed before the Academy

Awards and Ethan is my date. But I stayed quiet. Being clever on demand is hard!

Ethan started to speak to me but stopped. Then he said, "Tiernan, hey, call me when you're ready to hang out, and I can swing by later. Or tomorrow. Whatever."

He turned and left, not saying good-bye or even waving to me.

I felt a deflating sensation, like a balloon lost all its air in my chest.

He thought we sucked.

He's embarrassed for me.

He can't get the image of my face all puffed up yesterday out of his head.

He's going to go find Shelley and ask her out.

"Let's run through this one more time," Shane said, looking around the room.

"I have to go to the bathroom first," said Heidi. "Nina, come with me."

"Sure," I said, not feeling like playing anymore.

We went down the hall and found the bright blue bathroom, and Heidi flicked the overhead fan on and the tap full blast.

"I don't think anyone is listening to you go to the bathroom all the way down here," I said, confused.

"I don't have to have to go," Heidi said, giving me an impatient look.

"Then what are we doing in here?"

"You're being so weird to Ethan. You know he saved your life, right?"

"Wait, what?"

I'd changed the topic every single time any of my friends tried to tell me about the day at the farm, so I actually didn't really know what had happened. I was hoping to keep it that way. Anytime it came up, I felt both sick and horribly mortified. Awful times two!

"Yeah, he was the one who noticed you'd left and went to find out where you went. Then he came running back and got Mrs. Cook. And did I mention, that probably saved your life?"

"I didn't know that."

"Also, he likes you, dummy."

"No, Heidi, we've been friends forever. He doesn't *like me* like me. He just likes me. Besides, Shelley is into him and she's gorgeous."

"No, he likes you likes you. And he was worried about you being in the hospital. He called Tiernan twice that night to see if we'd heard from you. You could at least say 'thank you' to him."

With that, she turned off the tap and yanked opened the door, stomping out. I stood there, shocked. I knew she had to be wrong. Because I'd seen Ethan hanging out with Shelley all day at the farm, and she was clearly into him. And if my best friend from forever could dump me for Shelley after one meal all the way over in Italy, why wouldn't a cute boy choose her over me too? Especially considering how all over the place I'd been lately, like in a permanent state of confusion and awkward behavior.

I wish I knew what to think. After all those years of Brianna being bossy, I'd come to rely on having her help me figure out what to do all the time, even though anytime we talked about boys we had crushes on, she never acted like any of them might like me back.

But if Heidi was right, and Ethan liked me, it would be amazing. Because he was amazing. And being around him felt like the best Friday-before-spring-break feeling in the world. I smiled a little bit, secretly, just to myself.

The next morning, just as Mrs. Cook was about to dismiss us for first period, Principal Fontella's voice came on over the school intercom, sounding loud and scratchy.

"Please excuse the interruption," she started. "I wanted to remind everyone of a few upcoming events. One is the fund-raiser bake sale and fall festival this Saturday for the sixth grade whale-watching trip. Come on by and support your classmates on this very worthy cause.

"The second is something I'm personally very excited about. Our annual Halloween Talent Show, two weeks from Friday. Your teachers are going to hand in all sign-up forms at the end of the day today, so anyone who wants to show their classmates their incredible talent, be it singing, dancing, magic, or any other endeavor, today is your last opportunity to sign up."

A few kids groaned and laughed, but I saw Tiernan looking at me and giving me the thumbs-up sign. I smiled and shook my head at him. It was amazing how enthusiastic he always was about everything. It must be fun to be like that.

When the bell rang a minute later, Tiernan hopped up out of his chair and raced over to the form on Mrs. Cook's bulletin board and wrote down something. He gave me another thumbs-up. It was official. Our first live show!

Tiernan waved bye to me as I walked over to look at the sign-up sheet myself. I was curious to see if anyone else had added their names or if we were the only ones brave-slash-moronic enough to volunteer for public humiliation.

As I was staring, Shelley and Brianna walked up behind me.

"Are you going to be in the talent show?" Brianna said, "I thought you hated being on stage."

I shrugged, kind of embarrassed. "Yeah, I'm in a band."

"With who?" Shelley asked.

"It's, me, Tiernan, Madison, Shane, and Heidi."

"That's quite a group you've got there," Brianna said, smirking.

"You know, most seventh and eighth graders don't even go to the talent show," Shelley said, like she was doing me a big favor telling me that. "Last year my friends skipped it."

"Oh, that's okay, it's not about who comes, it's all

about playing for the fun of it," I said, feeling increasingly defensive.

"Also Brianna and I are having a huge party that night so we can't stop by the show because we have to get ready for our party. *It's a costume party.*" Shelley said that last part slowly, like it was a very important detail.

"Oh." I didn't know what else to say.

"The talent show will be kind of lame," Brianna added.

Was Brianna warning me, like trying to help me, or being mean to me about something I was *finally* doing on my own? Who could even tell with her anymore?

I was so confused and felt so embarrassed that I blurted out a world-record-level dumb comment.

"Kind of lame? The talent show is *totally* lame. It's, like, completely stupid, but I said I'd do it and now I have to. I don't want to at all. We're awful. I'm glad no one will be coming to see us, anyway."

"That is so harsh," Brianna laughed, but I felt like it was more with me than at me. Finally. It felt good to be included.

They walked off, waving to me.

I had no idea what had just happened but I felt like a huge liar for saying all those things about the Epis.

I took a deep breath, walked out the classroom, and

saw Tiernan standing there. He was staring at me. I smiled at him but he gave me a dirty look. He was furious. With me.

Because he'd overheard the whole thing.

"Seriously?" he said, the skin on his cheeks blotchy.

I looked down at my brown boots and noticed one toe was kind of scuffed and dirty.

"Nina, if you don't want to be in the band, forget it. We'll be fine without you."

"I was just joking, Tiernan!" I said, still looking anywhere but at him.

"That didn't sound like a joke." He was almost yelling, not caring that people passing by were staring.

"No, I really like being in the band. It's just...I'm not even sure why I said that."

"I know why. It's because you think you're too good for us. Exactly like you used to act all last year. I should have known you were still so shallow."

I swallowed hard, hunching up my shoulders. What could I possibly say? That my mouth had moved faster than my brain? That I was trying to fit in? That I was sorry and had been an idiot? I opened my mouth to speak, but Tiernan stormed off before I could say a word.

Over the next few hours, I had replayed the whole

incident in my head a hundred times over. My blurting out those mean comments about the band, Shelley and Brianna laughing, Tiernan looking so upset and hurt.

There was no way I could face him or any of The EpiPens now at lunch. Instead, I went to the nurse's office and asked that they call my mother to pick me up and take me home.

Mom looked worried when she came to get me at school in what seemed like record time.

"I'm fine, Mom," I told her for the fourth time as we got into the car.

"If you felt sick enough to go to the nurse, you're not fine. What's wrong?" Mom leaned over to put her hand on my forehead.

"I'm just tired," I said to her. That was true. I was exhausted. I couldn't believe the week I'd had.

When we got home, Mom insisted that I lie down on the couch so she could keep an eye on me. She kept busy in the kitchen but came out a few times. The first time she was carrying a mug of hot chocolate with a huge bunch of marshmallows. Then the next time she asked if I'd be "willing" to try out the new fudge recipe she'd been working on. "I'm going to call it 'Fudge Sludge,' because it looks like molten tar!"

Finally Mom announced that she just happened to

have all the ingredients to make veggie sushi rolls and
would I want that for lunch.

I love veggie sushi.

"Mom! Quit it!" I yelled.

"Quit what?" she said, looking innocent.

"You're making all my favorite foods. What's going
on? What's the catch?"

"No catch, honey. I'm just offering. I like cooking
for you."

"I don't even feel like eating," I said and put my head
back down on the orange-striped throw pillow.

"This hasn't been the best few weeks for you, has it?"
Mom patted my head. "Do you still feel tired?"

I sighed. "It's everything at school. I was trying to
get along with Brianna and I wound up hurting another
friend's feelings." I picked at the blue nail polish on my
thumb instead of looking at Mom.

"What happened?"

"It's too awful. I can't even go into it." I threw my nail
polish peel on the floor.

"Do you think you're overreacting? Things have a way
of blowing over."

I shrugged, like I didn't know, but I did know. There
was no blowing over on this one.

"I know things with Brianna haven't been good lately, and—"

"That's the understatement of the year," I interrupted her. I didn't want to talk about Brianna.

"Let me finish. I think it's actually a good thing that you're spending time with other classmates."

I looked at her. "Why?"

"Honey, this isn't about Brianna. It's about you. You have a lot to offer. You're funny. And kind. And smart. And talented. Maybe Brianna isn't the type of friend who is going to let you shine."

She leaned over to kiss me on the head and walked back into the kitchen.

Maybe Brianna had never let me shine, but at least I'd had backup 24/7. I had been making a giant mess out of flying solo.

The rest of my day was incredibly quiet. I checked my phone obsessively, but there were no calls or texts or anything from anyone in the band. What if they all hated me?

When I got to school the next morning, I actually felt like I might throw up. It seemed like the entire seventh grade

was in the lobby, hanging out and talking and having
fun. No one was waiting for me. If I never showed up
at Woodgrove Middle School again, I couldn't imagine
anyone would care.

Brianna and Shelley were on a bench with Josh in the
middle. He looked even dinkier next to two normal-sized
people. Ethan was standing sort of near them, bouncing a
soccer ball on his knee and talking to some other boys.

Tiernan was sitting with Shane and Madison. He
watched me as I walked toward him, but he acted like he
wasn't. I'd practiced the apology in my head over and over,
and how I'd explain I didn't mean it and was joking around,
but when I saw Tiernan again and remembered how
bummed he'd looked the day before, I realized the only possible thing I could say was "I'm sorry." Anything else would
sound like I was making an excuse, and there wasn't one.

Other than temporary insanity or temporary stupidity.

Except apologizing is so hard! And what if I did and
Tiernan was still mad and didn't want to forgive me? I'm
not sure I'd want to forgive me if I were him.

I pretended to be checking something on my phone as
I walked by Brianna and Shelley so I wouldn't have to talk
to them, but as I passed their bench, I heard Brianna say,
"Hi, Nina!" in a really loud voice.

Ethan looked around when he heard my name. He kept bouncing the soccer ball. He didn't smile or act happy to see me, like he usually did. Had I made him mad, somehow, too?

Wonderful.

"Hey," I said to Brianna, slowing down, even though I didn't want to. I wondered what she wanted.

"How's *the band*?" Brianna said.

Josh laughed.

Did she actually like me again because I'd acted mean and backstabby? She was awful.

Which made me even awfuler. All the time we were friends, I'd not only laughed whenever she'd made snarky comments about our classmates instead of sticking up for them, but I'd egged her on more times than I could bear to admit. Yesterday, as soon as I got even a slim glimmer of opportunity to be allowed back in her company again, I totally grabbed it.

I'd been obsessed with trying to get her to like me again. But what if I couldn't stand myself when I was around her?

I stopped walking and looked right at her.

"Thank you sooooo much for asking about the band," I said back, copying her fakey-face voice. "The Epis totally appreciate how into us you are. To answer your question, we are good. We rock."

Tiernan cracked a small smile—he'd heard me.

The bell rang and people began picking up their bags and filing out of the lobby. It was my chance to escape.

"Later," I said, trying to get the last word before she could say something rude to me.

"Are you *really* going to be in the talent show? With them?" She jutted her chin in the band's direction, not looking so nice now. "That is so lame."

"Why do you care what I do?" I was sick to death of trying to win her over, sucking up for a crumb of her attention.

"Please, I don't care. I'm just making conversation." She rolled her eyes.

"Make it with someone else, Brianna. I'm over your drama. Get over yourself."

She raised her eyebrows, surprised. Her mouth made an O shape, but she didn't say anything back to me.

Josh laughed loudly, and Brianna shoved him and said, "Shut up, idiot."

I did it!

My hands trembled a little.

I told Brianna off.

In all our years of being friends, I had never, not once, acted angry with her, even when I should have. I savored my victory, looking her straight in the eye one more time before I walked away.

So there!

I squared my shoulders and walked away like I didn't have a care in the world. It was a world-class acting job, because the past two minutes had been terrifying.

Now what?

I looked for Tiernan but he was gone, along with the rest of the band.

I raced up the stairs, looking for his curly hair in the crush of people.

"Tiernan," I gasped, spotting him. I grabbed him on the shoulder just before he went into the classroom. A few people gave me a funny look but whatever, I'd gotten plenty of those lately.

He turned around, surveying me warily.

"I'm sorry," I said. "I am so, so sorry. I was the worst yesterday."

"Eh, forget it," he said back, but instead of meeting my eyes, he kept rolling up the sleeves of his flannel shirt and then rolling them back down again. His nose looked red.

"I was…thoughtless."

"We aren't here to be playing backup for you, Nina. We're supposed to be your real friends, not second choice ones."

I felt my heart deflate a little and my eyes well up with tears.

"I like being in the band, Tiernan. Honestly. I told Brianna off just now. And I love you all. Not second best."

He smiled slightly. "We are a loveable, ragtag bunch."

"I was mean. And I won't do it again." I reached forward and gave him a hug before he could stop me.

"Hey, hey," he said, pushing me away and laughing. "Apology accepted."

Just then Mrs. Cook stuck her head out of the classroom. "Oh, excuse me. I thought you both might want to take part in educational matters, but don't let me stop you from whatever is clearly So. Much. More. Important."

Tiernan and I took one look at her face and hustled to our seats, covering our mouths so she wouldn't see us laughing. I felt magically lighter and happier—the load that had weighed me down for the past twenty-four hours gone. For once I didn't even mind risking Mrs. Cook's wrath.

I was walking into the cafeteria when I heard, "Nina, hold up." It was Ethan, catching his soccer ball behind his head with one arm so effortlessly he looked like an action hero or sports star. How come he always seemed so awesome at everything?

"Hey, Ethan."

"I asked Tiernan if you guys needed help with the band. You know, to help move equipment for the show."

Oh.

That was unexpected. Unexpectedly awesome!

By then we were standing in front of Tiernan and Madison and Shane.

"Ethan says he wants to help with the band," I told them.

"We could use the help," Madison said. "Even if you don't have any allergies, you're still allowed to be an EpiPen."

"I'm kind of sneezy around dust, does that count?" Ethan said.

"Hmm." I pretended to think it over.

Madison nodded. "Sure, sneezy counts," she said.

"Totally!" I got so excited about the idea of Ethan hanging out with the band that I gave his arm a squeeze, flirty Shelley style. Then I jumped back about ten feet like I'd done something weird. Which I had. But he smiled bigger anyway and rubbed his hair so it got all mussed up.

It made him look ridiculously cute.

"So when's the next practice? I should come too, right?" Ethan asked, standing slightly closer to me so that his gray and white sneaker touched the tip of my boot. Even though my boots were about three inches thick and padded with enough stuffing to fill a pillow, my whole foot got instantly warmer from the contact.

Ethan and Shane started talking, and Shane was entering his address into Ethan's phone.

Tiernan took a close-up picture without warning, the flash startling Ethan, leaving him blinking. "I'm going to send Heidi a photo of you while she's away so she knows we have a roadie."

Tiernan adjusted his phone. "Here, let me take another one. Shane, Madison, squeeze in there."

Ethan leaned in toward me, really close.

"Say 'Cheddar!'" Tiernan said.

"Cheddar!" We all yelled back.

Tiernan took another picture, but his flash didn't go off that time. I wondered if it was because my huge, goofy, grinning, beaming face was giving off enough light all on its own.

"Can I hang with you guys?" Ethan asked when he came back a few minutes later with his tray of chicken nuggets and other brown-colored food, bypassing his usual table of kids with Frisbees. "Am I even allowed to sit here, or do you, like, have to get permission?"

"Dude, you can eat. Relax," Tiernan said.

"Yeah, calm down, Ethan," Madison said. "We just sit here because we like each other. You won't kill us. Heidi doesn't have any allergies and she sits here and never gets into trouble."

"Agreed," I added. "You have to sit here. You're with the band now."

Ethan still looked tense. I would have felt bad for him, but I was too busy being happy that he was right there next to me.

"We just can't kiss someone after they've eaten a peanut," Madison said casually, as she was scribbling in her notebook.

Wait, what? Why was she talking about kissing all of a sudden?

"Yeah, it's kind of awkward," Shane said. "One time when we still lived in the city, I was at this school dance, and—"

"Hey, is that Principal Fontella riding a scooter?" I said, desperate to interrupt Shane. It was hard enough to get my nerve up to sit next to Ethan without anyone discussing making out.

"What?" everyone said, turning around to look in the direction I'd pointed.

"Oh, wait, false alarm, that's not her," I said, pretending to scan the room. "I must have been seeing things."

"So when is Heidi back again?" Shane said to Tiernan.

"Not until Tuesday."

"That doesn't give us much time to practice," Shane said. "I think we should get together without her, and then when she's back, she can jump in. Maybe we can call and put her on speakerphone so she can sing along."

"I'll ask her," Tiernan said, already texting. "But let's definitely practice tomorrow no matter what. I can't today because I have to go see Dr. Obvious. Ethan, my mom can give you a ride home afterward if you want. We usually ride to Shane's house on the bus after school."

"Do you bring your drums each time?" Ethan asked me.

"Mmmm. Wait, what?" I was confused because I wasn't listening. Instead I was looking at how cute Ethan was with his black tee. It was so new it was almost shiny and still had the creases where it had been folded.

"Oh, I mean, no, Shane's dad has a whole studio

downstairs with drums and everything. It's awesome. You'll see it tomorrow."

"Cool," Ethan said, bumping into me with his shoulder. On purpose.

"Yeah," I nodded, blushing. "Cool."

"Also, we should shoot our music video as soon as Heidi comes back," Shane said. "Something on a beach, maybe? With a bonfire? Or wait, no, at an abandoned old-timey carnival!"

"Shane, the nearest beach is about forty minutes away," Madison said. "And probably closed for the season. What do you mean carnival? Like, we're dressed up as clowns?"

"Maybe we should focus on learning the songs for the show," I added. "We're still not quite there yet. At least I need more practice."

"Okay, but we can't wait too long. A hot band's window is only open for a little while and then bam!" Shane slapped his hands together loudly, "It's over. You know, my dad is taking his new band to Ibiza over winter break to do a shoot. I bet we could tag along." He looked thoughtful and typed something on his phone.

Ethan looked at me, like trying to see if I thought Shane was crazy too. I just shook my head. Ethan had no idea what he was in for.

Chapter 17

Nina? Nina? Hey, Nina!"

Someone was nudging me in the shin with a hot pink, glitter- and paint-flecked sneaker.

I looked up at Madison, straightening iron in one hand, her blond hair pulled away from her head in the other. "Are you there? I asked you the same question five times!" Madison was looking at me funny.

"Sorry, I wasn't listening."

How could I listen to anything she said when my heart was beating so fast and so loud that it blocked out all other sounds? Could a twelve-year-old die from nerves? What was that thing—the vapors—in all the old stories? I had the vapors!

"I said, 'Do you want to borrow my straightener after I'm done?'" Madison spoke slowly.

I couldn't believe she was focusing on how her hair looked while I was busy freaking out about how I might self-combust on stage out of fear.

"Relax!" Madison smiled at me. "We're going to have fun."

Heidi looked at me and shook her head, a little of the glitter that she'd put in her hair shaking out with the movement. She and I both already discussed that Madison's lack of nerves was impressive, but also very, very bizarre.

Leslie, Madison's mom, who refused to let anyone call her by her last name, said she did "a lot of theater in college" and offered to do up all of the girls' makeup for the talent show. Heidi looked great—dramatic and rock-star-y, with white eyeliner and glitter on her cheekbones. I looked cool, in a way, but also strange—it wasn't my face staring back at me in the mirror. Plus my eyelashes felt all heavy from the mascara, like they were being weighed down. I kept blinking in confusion. I usually just wear lip gloss.

Madison's mom held out two bottles. "Nina, green or purple hair?"

"Green. But just a little!" I covered my face and held my breath while she sprayed away.

I looked at myself when she was done—I had one perfect streak on each side, framing my face. I felt a tiny peep of happy excitement in my chest pushing up against the scary peep.

Heidi skipped the streaks, and Madison picked a combo

of both—"Don't leave a single hair unsprayed," she told her mom. When Leslie was done, Madison looked like a stuffed animal come to life. Madison pronounced it "perfect."

Maybe we were going to be okay.

"We should get going," Leslie said. "You need time to get ready at school and to do your deep breathing exercises."

Apparently when you do drama stuff in college, taking long, slow breaths before any performance is a huge deal. Leslie was very into us screaming as loud as we could in order to find our "true primal voices" too. Whatever that meant.

We left Madison's room in total chaos, grabbing just what we needed before racing out to the car. All three of us squeezed into the back seat together.

Heidi's phone quacked. Madison and I turned to stare at her, and then we both dissolved into giggles. Heidi blushed.

"It's Tiernan. He wanted his own sound for when he texts me."

They were so cute it was ridiculous. Baby koala bears–level cute. Of course Tiernan would pick a duck and not, say, a loud motorcycle noise or a hit song or a burp.

I had to admit, I was kind of envious of them. They were a couple. Other than seeing Ethan when we were with everyone at school or practice, which, granted, was a lot, he and I hadn't done any hanging out just us two. And he hadn't called me since that one night after my allergic reaction nightmare.

He was super friendly to me, but he was like that to everyone. It was so hard to tell if he had a crush on me the way Heidi insisted he did, or only considered me a friend. In my mind, though, I always pretended that he did like me. It was a nice feeling. Beyond nice. An awesome one.

"Tiernan says the guys are already there and to hurry up," Heidi said, putting her phone back in her faded jean jacket pocket. With her skinny black jeans and black boots and her hair and makeup, Heidi looked like a real lead singer of a band. I just wore regular jeans and sneakers and a black long-sleeved tee. I debated something more "member of the band" and less "I'm hanging out with friends after school," but my dad pointed out that plenty of famous rock stars wear jeans and sneakers. I didn't look flashy, but I felt comfortable. Besides, with sneakers, I had added insurance that I wouldn't wipe out walking on or off the stage.

Just as I was thinking I wasn't scared anymore, we pulled up in front of the school. The parking lot was jammed full of cars. We couldn't find a spot, and Leslie had to pull up in front of the building to let us out so she could drive around again to park. I couldn't believe it. Who were all these people, anyway? I thought the talent show was considered a big non-event.

The joke's on me. I'd been counting on an audience of max fifteen or twenty people. Not a hundred. Was I going to throw up? Way to cap an already cringe-worthy few weeks.

When Madison, Heidi, and I opened the doors to the lobby, people turned to look at us.

"Whoo!" yelled someone—I couldn't see who—from the crowd.

"They look great," I heard someone else say to the person next to her. I couldn't figure out who was who, even though I'd been going to school with these people forever.

"Guys, I am nervous. About to barf nervous." I grabbed Heidi's hand and squeezed.

"Nina! Over here!" Ethan suddenly appeared out of nowhere. Like magic. I remember my grandma telling me once that when she was a girl and thought a boy was cute, she and her friends would say he was "dreamy." Could there be a more perfect word for Ethan than that?

"Come with me," he said. "Shane and Tiernan are backstage already checking out the amps and the drum set we got from the band room." He took my hand and pulled me, and we all ran down the auditorium aisles, and Ethan took the steps to the stage two at a time. I had to let go of his hand so I could take them one at a time though.

Stumbling—not very rock star.

He turned to wait for me and smiled. I was too nervous to smile back. He reached out and took my hand again. This time it wasn't because he needed to pull me through the crowd. This time it was because he wanted to take my hand. Unless I looked like I was going to faint and he was just worried about me. But I really didn't think so anymore. No one is *that* nice.

I took a deep, cleansing breath like Leslie had taught us. "Feel it from your head down to your toes. Get energy from the earth," she'd explained. I coughed—I guess I'd cleansed out a bit too much.

"Nina, come on!" Heidi waved to me. The rest of the band was waiting too, along with Shane's dad.

"We're on eighth," Shane said, brandishing a clipboard. We all clustered around him. There were twelve acts total listed.

"That's perfect," Shane's dad said. "You'll have the audience just where you want them. Ready for something to shake things up a bit but not restless to go home."

I wasn't so sure that made sense, but whatever. Mr. McCormick certainly knew more than the rest of us about this stuff. If he said eight was lucky, then I was going to cross my fingers that he was right.

Ms. Sherf, the band teacher, was clapping her hands and trying to get everyone's attention. "People, people, listen up! We can't have everyone milling about backstage for the whole show. Go find seats in the audience, and make your way here when you're two acts away. That's two, not three or one! We'll let the audience in in five minutes, so please get yourselves situated as far forward as possible to avoid disruptions."

"Come on, let's grab our seats now," Tiernan said, and we all trooped out from behind the stage to the auditorium, along with a bunch of the other kids who'd been backstage with us too, including one sixth grade girl in a magician's cape and an eighth grade boy wearing a fancy suit and sneakers.

The EpiPens got seats in the second row, all together. I sat in between Madison and Heidi, who sat next to Tiernan. I'd wanted to sit with Ethan, but I didn't want to seem obvious about it. Sometimes in my quest to avoid looking stupid, I do really stupid things. The good thing at least was if I had a full-on freak out, he wouldn't notice.

The doors opened, and a wave of sound made its way through the auditorium. I turned around to stare—and to look for my parents or Jackson. It seemed like the entire school had shown up for the night.

"Oh. My. God." Heidi mouthed to us.

"Why are so many people here?" Madison said. "The talent show wasn't ever this huge before, was it?"

"I told you guys!" Shane said, looking smug. "Word of mouth, baby, word of mouth."

Just then I saw Jackson, who started waving his arms, yelling, "Mom, I found her, she's right here!"

"Shh!" I said, but nobody really noticed him; it was way too loud in the auditorium. Mom and Dad came up to my row. Mom was holding flowers that I knew were for me, because they were yellow tulips, my favorite.

"Hi, guys." I was relieved to see them. At least three people would be cheering for us.

"We're sitting right back there," Mom said, pointing toward the middle of the auditorium. "It sure is crowded here. How exciting."

"Right? I can't believe it either," I said. Not sure exciting was the word I would have chosen.

"Have a great show. We'll find you when it's over. May the rock be with you!" Dad said, patting me on the shoulder, and they all walked back up the aisle to their seats.

The lights dimmed, and one person whistled super

loud, which made people laugh. Finally it got quiet. Principal Fontella came out onto the stage, wearing black pants and a blazer instead of her normal gray skirt suit. She didn't even look principal-y.

"Welcome, everyone, to the annual Woodgrove Halloween Talent Show. We're so thrilled to see such a wonderful turnout. Please, let's take a moment to thank Ms. Sherf for helping organize this event, and for being the emcee for the evening."

The audience applauded politely as Ms. Sherf walked out on to the stage and took the microphone.

"Thank you, Principal Fontella. We have so many talented students here tonight, so let's get right to it. Let's give a warm welcome to our first act, Robert Wilcox, who will share his comedy with us."

The kid wearing the suit came out on stage, holding what looked like an unlit cigar.

"Thanks, everyone. I just flew in from California, and boy, are my arms tired." I slunk down in my seat and closed my eyes.

Don't throw up. Don't throw up.

I kept them squeezed shut during the second act too ("Magic by Margaret") and third ("CheerUp!") with what sounded like about eighteen girls on stage yelling. The audience actually applauded for each act—maybe they weren't giving standing ovations or acting like their lives were forever changed, but at least no one was hurling spit-balls or yelling, "BOO!" at anyone. That was promising.

I looked around again. People were having fun. I couldn't believe how well things were going so far.

The sixth act ("Al Cap 'n' Ella") took the stage—three eighth graders who sang "Landslide" with no instruments. They sounded incredible.

Crap.

"Guys, come on!" Tiernan was whispering to us as the audience applauded "Al Cap 'n' Ella," and they started to sing another song that I didn't recognize. "We have to go backstage and get ready."

We got up and snuck to the side of the auditorium and backstage. I heard a few people whisper behind us as we went. "What are they going to sing?" and "Is that them?"

Them who? Wait, them, us? No way!

Act number seven ("A Poem by Duane") was intro-duced, but I couldn't hear much of what he was saying over the sound of my breathing and beating heart.

"Group hug," Madison said, pulling everyone closer. We all hugged.

"Go Epis!" Shane said, giving high fives and fist bumps

to each of us. We heard applause. Ms. Sherf hurried us along—we grabbed our instruments, with Ethan helping, and Tiernan slung his guitar over his shoulder. We were as ready as we'd ever be.

"Our next act is the band, The EpiPens, singing 'Cruel to be Kind.' Welcome, EpiPens! We hope the audience won't be cruel, but they'll be kind to you." Ms. Sherf laughed at her own joke. That was so not how they intro bands at the MTV Music Awards.

The crowd got quiet. The curtain went up. I couldn't see into the audience at all—not Mom or Dad or anyone.

"Ready?" I said, my voice only trembling a tiny bit, as I turned to make sure my band mates were all set. I clicked my sticks once, but then Tiernan yelled, "Wait!"

I froze.

His guitar strap had come undone, and I saw him struggling to snap it back on. Heidi stepped over to help him, and I heard a few giggles from the audience. Tiernan seemed flustered, and when he said, "Okay, now we're ready," his voice cracked a little.

I looked around at them and nodded. My hands were shaking so hard I was worried I wouldn't be able to drum, but I clicked my sticks four times, and we launched into the song.

I got snippets of music and sound and images—Heidi hitting her notes, Tiernan's head moving along with his playing, but it all happened so fast I didn't even have time to think—just drum. And then we were done, and I couldn't believe it. Had I even had time to breathe once?

There was a moment and then everyone in the auditorium started to applaud, like not the so-so way they did with "CheerUp!" but super loud and excited. The lights came up and I could see people standing and yelling. We'd done it!

One more? Shane mouthed to us, and as the crowd kept clapping, we sang our second song, "Bitter Little Shame Puppet," by The Flax Seeds.

I admit, the song wasn't quite as awesome as "Cruel to be Kind," but it gave Madison an opportunity to do her flute solo. She totally rocked it. When she started playing, people were, like, screaming and stomping their feet and acting like the flute was the coolest thing around. Madison didn't seem fazed at all by the reaction. She just finished her solo, and we all launched into the final verse.

When it was over and the audience was cheering, we walked off the stage without even taking a bow or turning to acknowledge the crowd, which we'd planned ahead of time, because Shane said it was cooler to "love them and leave them" than to stay and bask in our glory like fame hogs.

We got backstage, and for a minute, no one said anything. We just stared at each other in shock.

"We killed it," Shane said finally, breaking into the biggest smile I'd ever seen on his face. "We really did it."

"GROUP HUG!" Madison shouted again, and we all grabbed each other and held on. I felt like I was having a weird dream. It was over? That was it? I couldn't believe we'd gotten up there, rocked it, and now all our weeks of practice were done and we could just...well, I wasn't sure what we could do, but my not waking up with a giant ball of panic in my stomach was certainly top of my list.

"I didn't throw up!" I shouted, squeezing everyone extra tight. "Yeah, us! You guys were all so amazing."

Ms. Sherf came up to us. "Listen to your fans," she said, actually sounding excited. "Great job!"

Then she shooed us back into the audience. "Now, go sit and listen to the rest of the acts and don't forget to applaud."

We went back to our seats. The yellow tulips were

waiting, perched on top of my jacket, and there was a yellow tulip on the chairs where Madison and Heidi had been sitting before too. Mom must have snuck them down and put them there for us.

Ethan was in the aisle too. He shoved a slightly squished red rose in a plastic wrapper into my hand. It was the most perfect flower ever.

"You were great," he whispered.

"Is that for me?" I said, as Shane and Madison squeezed in past us. "Thank you."

Wow.

"Sit down!" we heard someone say behind us, and Ethan and I grabbed the two seats at the end of the aisle. I held onto my flowers on my lap, the rose laying carefully on top of the bouquet of tulips. I felt like a star.

Someone behind us patted me on the shoulder and said, "Good job!"

I turned around. It was an eighth grader I didn't know.

"Thanks," I said, beaming.

The final act finished ("Dog Tricks with Almond and Paisley"), and then Principal Fontella was thanking everyone for coming and asking us to please be careful exiting the parking lot.

"Now what?" Tiernan said, turning to us.

"Um, now I go home and pass out for the rest of the weekend. That was intense," Heidi said, laughing. "I'm exhausted."

"No way, we're doing a victory lap. Let's hit that Halloween party," Shane said. "My dad can give us a ride; he's got the van he uses to load his equipment."

"No, no, no," Madison said. "I don't want to hang out with Shelley and Brianna. They've been walking around for weeks acting like they invented costume parties. They are going to be unbearable to be around."

"Yeah, anyway, I don't have a costume," Ethan said. "We should skip it."

So it was officially official. Ethan wasn't into Shelley. Otherwise he'd definitely want to go to her party. *And* he gave me a rose.

Could my night get any better?

"I think we should go too," Tiernan said. "Shane's right—we deserve a victory lap and it's either that or go to the diner and order fries. Not that there's anything wrong with that."

"Did everyone get amnesia and forget that I told Brianna off? And that she hasn't spoken to me since?" I said.

"I'm not going if you're not," Ethan said.

"I'm not going if they're not," Madison added.

"Come on! It's the only after party around. We're going. I can't go home after a show. It's epically lame." Shane even added a pathetic sounding "Please? This is our big night!"

Shane never says please.

Everyone looked at me.

"Stop staring, guys!" I yelled, half laughing.

Mom and Dad and Jackson came through the crowd.

"Thanks for the flower, Mrs. Simmons," Madison said, hugging my mom. Mom looked surprised—but in a nice way.

"Yeah, Mom, thanks," I said. I reached over to hug her and Dad and even Jackson.

Dad wiped his eyes. Was he crying? Oh, no!

"Dad!"

"I'm fine. I seem to have come down with a slight head cold," he said, blowing his nose on a tissue. He was lying though.

"That was amazing. The EpiPens were the best of the whole show," Mom said. She looked proud.

"Right?" Tiernan said. "So, Nina, are you coming with us to that party?"

Mom looked at me. "Whose house? Will their parents be there?"

I shrugged. I knew Shelley must have parents, but she seemed so sophisticated I kind of imagined her living on her own, or maybe she'd hatched fully formed, or been sent by aliens to infiltrate and take over our civilization.

"My dad made me check," Heidi said. "Shelley's mother will be there."

Mom looked at Dad. Dad looked at Mom. Finally, she shrugged.

"Well," she said. "Do you want to go? We can give you a ride."

"No, that's okay. Shane's dad has a van that fits everyone, right?" I looked to Shane for confirmation. "I mean, if we even decide we're going."

I realized, as I was talking, that maybe I did want to go. I wanted Brianna to see that I was fine. And I wasn't afraid of what she'd say anymore.

And that way the night didn't have to end. I was in a band that rocked and a boy that I'd liked for what felt like forever, miraculously, seemed to like me back. Who could go home after that?

"Is that okay?" I asked, looking at my parents.

"It's fine. Call us when you want to get picked up. Before eleven thirty!"

Eleven thirty? Way to make me look cool, Mom.

But all I said was, "Got it, Mom."

She resisted giving me a second hug. I could tell it took all her willpower though. When my parents and Jackson walked away, I heard Jackson ask, "Could I take drums too?" It was nice that he actually wanted to copy something cool I was doing instead of copying getting attention from a doctor. Hopefully he'd stop talking about weird illnesses now, although that wasn't likely.

"So we're doing this?" Shane said. "Awesome. Let me find my dad."

"I'm not wearing a costume," Ethan said. "I hate costumes."

"It's fine, none of us are," Madison said.

"Yeah, but you guys look like rock stars," said Ethan, high-fiving Tiernan.

"Well, you can tell everyone you're dressed as a roadie, then," I said.

Like Shelley would care what Ethan was dressed like. She'd never give him a hard time for showing up uncostume-y. I hoped Brianna wouldn't be mad if I came. Although if she was, I'd just avoid her and hang out with the band.

"You don't feel weird about coming with us, right, Nina?" Tiernan said, only loud enough for me to hear.

"Not at all, Tiernan. I promise." And I meant it.

Shane's dad dropped us off at Shelley's house and then took off with a fist out the window, shouting, "Rock on, kids."

There were a bunch of our classmates there, and when we walked in the door, a ton of people started clapping and yelling. Tiernan was waving to everyone and bowing and acting like a goof, like always.

Shelley came through a swinging door, probably from the kitchen. She had on a black T-shirt and black shorts, and knee-high black boots. Basically, she was dressed up to look hot. The only tipoff she was in an actual costume was the witch hat on her head.

"Oh, hi!" she said, looking a bit surprised at seeing all of us. "Everyone says you guys were really…good."

"Check it out—they were great," Ethan said, pulling out his phone. He started the video of us playing, and some people clustered around him to see it.

"That's cool," Shelley said, then wandered off, uninterested.

I walked away from Ethan and his phone. I didn't think I could bear to watch myself so soon—what if we hadn't been as great as I'd thought, or I'd made stupid drummer faces during the performance and hadn't realized it? I took a few steps backward, away from the music, almost bumping into someone.

"Oh, hi, Nina."

It was Brianna, wearing the identical costume to Shelley. Big shock. That was so Brianna's style—her and her best friend as a team against the world. I couldn't believe I'd thought that was so great for so many years.

"Um, great party," I said, shoving my hands into the pockets of my jeans.

"Yeah, pretty major, right?"

"Yep, totally major."

She shrugged. "I have kind of more important things to do right now. See you around."

I watched as Brianna walked away, feeling relieved more than anything else. A few months ago, if there'd been a party, we'd have planned to go together and stayed by each other's sides the whole time. I probably hadn't made a decision to go somewhere without her for years. Standing by myself in the middle of a big, loud, crowded room—I felt like I'd accomplished something amazing.

Yeah, I still kind of missed having a best friend, but it was nice having a life I could call my own.

I wasn't alone for long. Ethan was walking toward me, pushing up the sleeves on his long-sleeved tee.

"Hey," he said. "People can't get enough of The EpiPens, see?" He motioned toward Shane, who was showing "Cruel to be Kind" to another group of kids.

"How's the roadie costume? Anyone guess what you were?"

"Not so much. I won't be winning any best dressed prizes tonight," Ethan said.

"Oh, hi, you two!" Shelley said, appearing by our side. She held a cup up close to Ethan's face, balancing herself perfectly on her super high heels. "You want?"

"What is that?" Ethan said.

"Tiramisu, from a bakery in the city. Like, the best bakery ever."

"No thanks," I said. "It looks amazing. But I'm all set."

Ethan leaned in to me and bumped my shoulder with his. "None for me, either."

Shelley walked off, as cheerfully as she'd come up, offering the cups to the next group. I'd spent the past two months feeling so mad at Shelley for stealing Brianna away from me and assuming that her flirting with Ethan was some malicious act against me, but now I didn't feel a speck of anger toward her.

Ethan smiled at me. "What?" I said, feeling self-conscious. I rubbed my nose. Did I have something hanging out of it?

He leaned in closer to me.

What was happening?

Then I wasn't thinking about Shelley, or The EpiPens, or anything else anymore.

He kissed me quickly on the lips—it kind of landed half on my chin, but I didn't care. Ethan smelled dreamy—like soap and general awesomeness.

He touched his forehead to mine and looked into my eyes. "Shane is right. Girl drummers rule," he said.

I started giggling.

"What's so funny?" Madison said, coming up to us with Heidi and Tiernan.

I didn't answer. I was too happy to even speak.

I had become someone who had been kissed! And by a guy I liked, not, like, kissed on a dare by someone disgusting.

"Where's Shane?" Heidi said. "We need the whole band together so we can get a photo."

"He's right there, planning on taking over the charts," Tiernan said, motioning to where Shane stood typing on his cell phone, oblivious to the sea of people around him.

"I can't believe the night is over," I said. "I'm still in shock!"

Shane came up to join us.

"Yo," he said. "I was just talking to my dad. He sent our video to The Flax Seeds and he said they were going to send it out to their followers. I'm telling you, we can totally get a sponsor and make a video. I'm sure of it."

"Shane, come on, let's just chill for the rest of the night. This rock star needs a break. And a giant bottle of water. My throat is killing me," Heidi said.

"I'll go with you to find some." I couldn't wait to tell Heidi that Ethan had kissed me. Normally when someone says "I told you so" to me, I get annoyed, but this would be the best "I told you he liked you" ever.

"Do you want me to bring water back for you too?" I asked Ethan, blushing a little.

Madison and Heidi gave me looks like they knew what was going on.

"People, before you go get drinks, we need photos, and one more hug," Madison said.

Ethan put his arm around my shoulder, and we all squeezed up close together for a picture.

"Go Epis," he said.

"Go Epis!" we all yelled as the light flashed.

NINA'S FAVORITE BREAKFAST SMOOTHIE

From the cookbook *Allergy-Free Mornings*, by
Claudia Simmons and Nina Simmons

INGREDIENTS:

  1 ripe banana

  1 cup coconut milk

  1 cup diced strawberries

  Ice

  Agave nectar

DIRECTIONS:

  Puree the banana, coconut milk, and strawberries in a
  blender.

  Add ice 1–2 cubes at a time until you get the right
  consistency.

  Add agave nectar to taste and give one more quick
  blend. Ta-da!

SERVES 2

Acknowledgments

Many thanks to my wise and patient first draft readers Emma, Holly, Lorelei, and Sarah, and for the additional feedback by Leonard, Danielle, Kate, Miriam, Eliana and Edie, Tara, Patty, Eric, and Nora. So appreciate getting a kick-start courtesy of The Book Doctors and their fabulous Pitchapalooza event at Oblong Books & Music (best bookstore ever!). And thank you Erica Rand Silverman for your wisdom and support. To Aubrey Poole and the Sourcebooks team who helped bring *My Year of Epic Rock* to life, much gratitude. I'm so glad we're in this together.

About the Author

Andrea Pyros is an experienced writer and former teen magazine editor. She's also had jobs waiting tables (hard!), baking cookies (delicious!), steaming clothing (hot!), and interviewing celebs (terrifying!). But other than a brief period wanting to be a private detective like Nancy Drew or Trixie Belden, she's dreamt of being a writer all her life. A native of New York City, she now lives in New York's Hudson Valley with her husband and their two children. This is her first novel. Visit her at www.andreapyros.com.